When David Died

A True Story

By
John Locke

This book is a work of fiction. Names, characters, places and incidents are either the product of the author's imagination or are used fictitiously. Any resemblance to actual persons, living or dead, or to actual events or locales is entirely coincidental.

WHEN DAVID DIED

The publisher does not have any control over and does not assume any responsibility for author or third-party websites or their content.

Cover Designed by: Claudia Jackson
Copyright © iStock_13231103

Published by John Locke Books, LLC

Visit the author's website:
http://www.donovancreed.com

ISBN 978-1-937656-03-4 (eBook)
ISBN 978-1-937656-04-1 (paperback)

Version 2016.08.20

Personal Message from John Locke:

I love writing books, but what I love even more is hearing from readers. If you enjoyed this or any of my other books it would mean the world to me if you'd click the link below so you can be on my notification list. That way you can receive updates, contests, prizes, and savings of up to 67% on eBooks immediately after publication!

Just access this link: http://www.DonovanCreed.com and I'll personally thank you for trying my books.

Also, if you get a chance, I hope you'll check out my friend Dani Ripper's website:

http://www.DaniRipper.wordpress.com

John Locke

New York Times Best Selling Author

Guinness World Record Holder for eBook Sales!

8th Member of the Kindle Million Sales Club!

(Members include James Patterson, George R.R. Martin, and Lee Child)

John Locke had 4 of the top 10 eBooks on Amazon/Kindle at the same time, including #1 and #2!

...Had 6 of the top 20 books <u>at the same time!</u>

...Had 8 books in the top 43 <u>at the same time!</u>

...Has written 30 books in five years in <u>six separate genres, All best-sellers!</u>

...Has been published throughout the world in numerous languages by the world's most prestigious publishing houses!

...Winner, Second Act Magazine's Story of the Year!

...Named by Time Magazine as one of the "Stars of the DIY-Publishing Era"

Wall Street Journal: "John Locke (is) transforming the 'book' business"

John Locke

New York Times Best Selling Author
#1 Best Selling Author on Amazon Kindle

Donovan Creed Series:

Lethal People
Lethal Experiment
Saving Rachel
Now & Then
Wish List
A Girl Like You
Vegas Moon
The Love You Crave
Maybe
Callie's Last Dance
Because We Can!
This Means War!

Emmett Love Series:

Follow the Stone
Don't Poke the Bear
Emmett & Gentry
Goodbye, Enorma
Rag Soup
Spider Rain

Dani Ripper Series:

Call Me!
Promise You Won't Tell?
Teacher, Teacher
Don't Tell Presley!
Abbey Rayne

Dr. Gideon Box Series:

Bad Doctor
Box
Outside the Box
Boxed In!

Other:

Kill Jill
Casting Call
When David Died

Kindle Worlds:

A Kiss for Luck (Kindle Only)

Non-Fiction:

How I sold 1 Million eBooks in 5 Months!

Dedication:

To all the independent authors in the world
who deserve to be read:

You're the true champions!
Keep fighting the fight,
and don't let anyone steal your dream!

When David Died

A True Story

Very Important: Please read!

You may have noticed the title page states: "This book is a work of fiction."

I thought long and hard about removing that tag, but finally deferred to the advice of my attorneys after one of the participants depicted in this book threatened a seven-figure lawsuit to stop publication. While I'm not the least bit concerned about losing the case, the courts could have tied up my manuscript for years, during which time some other writer or reporter might be the one to bring the story to the public. So while it annoys the shit out of me to not *officially* tag this book as non-fiction, I realize my attorneys are simply doing their jobs, trying to protect me, and I'd be a fool not to follow their legal advice.

When movies include the tagline *Based on a True Story* it usually means two things: there *is* a true story, and this isn't it! But I'm writing books, not screenplays, and therefore have more opportunities, more *space*, to make certain the account is supremely accurate.

Even so, this story isn't 100% true. Although the police detectives' notes, interviews, and final report are a matter of public record, the names and settings are fictitious and the internal and external dialogues of the characters are my best attempt (based on interviews and source material) to recreate what I believe was thought and said by them at the time.

My attorneys have further advised me to point out that certain portions of the narrative rely on a series of in-person interviews I may or may not have paid for that were conducted with the major player in this story, aka Nicki Hill.

To date, surprisingly, no one has been arrested for any actions depicted within these pages.

Forward

We all have secrets. Big ones, small ones, life-changing ones.

They say knowledge is power. But I say if you *really* want to destroy people, do two things: learn their secrets, and exploit them.

Part One:

Nicki Hill

Chapter 1

MID NOVEMBER

Wednesday
5:50 p.m.

IF YOU'RE THE cute couple that just entered the Hurstbourne Starbucks you're watching Michael and me laughing our asses off. We've been talking about something he read on the Internet about how to make his kitchen smell great. "Heat the oven to 300," he said, "put two capfuls of vanilla extract in an oven-proof bowl, cook it for 30 minutes."

"Doesn't work," I said.

"You tried it?"

"Yup. And believe me—Wait. Did you say two *cap* fulls?"

He nodded.

"Oops. I thought it was two *cup* fulls! No wonder for six weeks my house smelled like the Pillsbury Dough Boy's butthole!"

It wasn't original, but we laughed ourselves stupid anyway, because laughter always hitchhikes with happiness, and our relationship is currently in a good place. He's happy I'm back; I'm happy my life's on track. It took the better part of a year, but...my future finally appears secure, and even—if I'm not getting ahead of myself—limitless.

Three months ago the handsome man sitting across from me—twenty-one-year-old Michael Thorne—asked me to marry him.

It's not what you think: I said no. Then I broke up with him, moved out, and now I'm back and we're no longer talking about marriage or having kids, which is what broke us up in the first place. Back in those days (three months ago) Michael was confused: "You said family's the most important thing in the world!"

"It is," I said.

"Then what's changed?"

"Nothing. I just don't want to have children."

"Are you saying you want to adopt?"

"No."

"Then what the fuck *are* you saying, Nicki?"

It went like that for a while, and then I moved out. Then I talked to his mom, Alison, and his sister, Jessie, and then I talked to his dad, David.

And now I'm back.

Here's what we worked out: I agreed to let him tell people we're engaged, and he agreed not to ask me about setting a wedding date. From my perspective, this took the pressure off the relationship, and we're getting along famously, and it's a Wednesday evening, and we're sitting in a coffee shop, and his phone's ringing.

He checks caller ID and sighs. "It's Mom."

I stand. "Tell her I love her."

He grins. "Will do. Where are you going?"

I point to the counter. "Cranberry scone. Want one?"

"Vanilla," he says, and I walk to the counter and get in line behind two teenagers who can't decide between the Caramel Waffle Cone Crème Frappuccino Blended Crème and the Double Chocolaty Chip Crème Frappuccino Blended Crème.

They're happy, I'm happy, we're all happy.

I've been through a lot. Come so freaking far. Persevered. Am I proud of everything I did to get to this point?

Of course not.

Then again, courtships are tough, and what woman *hasn't* said or done things she wouldn't brag about while trying to secure her future happiness? Maybe she omitted certain details about her past, like her drug history, her ex-lovers, or the fact she's actually two years older than her fiancé. Maybe she didn't want sex or wasn't ready for it but gave herself to him anyway, to keep from losing him. Maybe she exaggerated her feelings for him because she never had a family and fell in love with his. Or maybe she broke up with him knowing it would make him crazy for her, knowing if she gave him another chance he'd be so glad to have her back he'd stop talking about having kids.

The sudden noise behind me is like something out of a horror film. I turn to see Michael standing, shaking, sobbing. I bolt to his side, shouting, "Michael! What on earth?"

"My father's dead."

"*What?*"

"He *hanged* himself."

The room starts spinning. I grab my stomach, fight to keep from vomiting. "*Omigod! Omigod!* Oh *no!*"

He sits beside me, grabs me and holds on for dear life, and we rock back and forth and sob together on the floor, completely ignoring the manager and customers surrounding us, who ask if there's something they can do. We've gone from top of the world to the depths of despair in seconds and the one thing I know with absolute certainty is things will never be the same. All the plans and sacrifices I've made have just gone up in flames. And yet...as I think about it, I wonder if there might yet be a silver lining.

Over the next two hours we're in a slow-motion fog. I literally can't remember getting to our feet, leaving the coffee shop, walking back to Michael's apartment. Even now, we're in a daze: packing clothes, stopping to cry, calling our bosses, stopping to cry, calling his mom, calling his sister, stopping to cry. Now, standing at the threshold of his bedroom, bags in hand, we take a moment to look at the clothes strewn throughout the room.

"You have everything you need?" he says.

"Yes."

"Okay then, we should get going. Mom and Jess need us."

I nod, knowing the next few hours and days will be extremely difficult. Over the past year I've grown extremely close to Michael's family, and while I want to be all in for them, my mind's going a thousand miles an hour, fighting the urge to bail. Because if David left a suicide note...

Michael doesn't know, because other than the *means* of death, Alison refused to give any details over the phone.

"It's impossible," Michael says as I watch the trees and houses fly past the car window. "In a million years Dad would never kill himself."

He's right. David wouldn't.

Except that he *did*.

And though I'm as shocked as anyone, I might be the only person on Earth who knows why he did it.

Unless he left a note, in which case the whole world will know by this time tomorrow.

As we work our way toward Lexington I make a mental note to ditch my secret cell phone at the first opportunity.

Chapter 2

8:15 p.m.

THE THORNE ESTATE was carved from a parcel of Fairborn Farms that was sold to generate quick cash in the early 1990's when the thoroughbred business was suffering major losses. When the investor died his children subdivided the parcel and David Thorne purchased the largest tract, approximately nine acres, for $2 million. On that piece of prime land, he built the 15,000 square foot mansion we're currently approaching, and it was here that Michael first introduced me to his family 16 months ago. Behind the house is a huge gazebo that overlooks a sculptured pond. Seven months ago, after breaking up with Michael, I sat on one of the gazebo benches with Alison to explain why family was so important to me: "I was a ward of the state, shuffled from one foster family to the next. I never had a proper childhood with sisters and brothers and loving parents."

Alison said, "Michael shared that much with us before your first visit. And since that time we've grown to love you like a daughter."

"I know, and I'm 100% grateful. I love you too."

John Locke

"It's a marvel how well you turned out given your rough start. It speaks to your character and determination."

"Thank you."

"I'm serious, Nicki. I don't know anyone who could have handled all you've been through and come out with such a positive attitude. I really admire that, and how you always made the best out of whatever situation you found yourself in. Those are the types of qualities that make a marriage work." She paused, then said, "Would you consider telling me about your aversion to having children?"

I looked at her a minute, then took a deep breath and said, "At 10:15 on the night of the best birthday I ever had, my foster father took my virginity at knife-point, even while his wife tapped on the door to whisper she loved me. I was fourteen, a year younger than Jessie, if that helps put it in perspective."

"Oh my *God*, Nicki! That's horrible! I'm so sorry."

"It's okay. He wasn't the first foster parent to molest me. He just took things up a notch. Later on I caught a lucky break after they arrested him for murdering one of his other foster daughters, who happened to be my best friend in the house. If I'd been home that morning, it could have been me."

Alison shook her head, sadly. "That may be the worst childhood story I've ever heard. But can I ask you something? How does that experience relate to your not wanting children?"

"My insides got so messed up the doctors doubt I can get pregnant. And if I do, they said I could die trying to give birth."

"Was the rape that brutal? Even with your foster mother close by in the house that night?"

"No ma'am. But the abortion was." As Alison hung on my words and watched me through wide eyes I added, "It was the first he ever performed."

"The doctor?"

7

"My foster father."

"Jesus, Nicki. I'm so sorry."

"It's all right. Like you said, I was determined to have a better life."

"Well, thank God you finally got away from that family."

"I did. But just when I thought that was as bad as things could get, I was placed with the Davenports. Please don't ask me what happened there, okay?"

She nodded.

"Not ever!"

We hugged a long time, and she said, "Have you told any of that part to Michael?"

I looked down at my hands. "No."

"I'm sure it would help him understand your feelings."

"I know. But he really wants kids, and should have them. It's why I had to leave. I just don't want children."

"Nicki, I'm sure he loves you much more than he wants children. And don't forget, you can always adopt."

"True. But during the breakup he said some pretty harsh things to me."

She took my hand in hers and smiled. "We save our harshest comments for the ones we love the most. I know you've had a terrible life up till now, but you and Michael are still so very young. It's just natural you're going to make mistakes and have some bumps along the way. You should give him another chance, Nicki. He adores you."

"I know. Can I ask you something?"

"Anything."

"Do you have any regrets?"

That caught her by surprise. "About what?"

"I don't know. I mean, like you said, Michael and I are pretty young, and this is a big decision. I guess I'm wondering if you regret any decisions you made, or didn't make."

She thought about it for a moment, then said, "Nothing major comes to mind."

"Even when you were my age? Or younger? Was there anything you wanted to do that you didn't? Or, thinking back on it, was there anything you would have done differently if you had the chance?"

She smiled. "Such a serious question!"

"I'm sorry. I know that was terribly personal."

"Not at all," she said. "I've been very fortunate. Whether on purpose or by accident, I'm pretty comfortable with the decisions I've made. So far, at least."

"So, no regrets?"

"Not really. Nothing worth mentioning. But Nicki? Try not to put too much pressure on yourself. Take your time. Don't force the decision. For now, just agree to think about getting back with Michael."

"Okay."

She kissed my cheek. "Michael's not the only Thorne who loves you, Nicki. We *all* do. And if things don't work out between you guys, I hope you know we'll always consider you part of the family. I'm sure Michael will, too."

I hugged her like she saved my life, then asked, "Would it be okay if I call David sometime this week to get his perspective about how Michael views our future?"

"That's a good idea. I'm sure he'd be glad to take your call."

"What about Jessie?"

"Jessie?"

"Before I head back to Louisville I'd like to reassure her that no matter what happens with Michael I'll always be there for her."

"That's so thoughtful!" she said. "Of course you should tell her that."

And so I did, and it was the last time I stepped foot on these grounds until tonight. Now, exiting Michael's car, we find our path blocked by a police detective named Broadus, who tells us we can't enter the house until the police conclude their initial investigation.

"I'm the son," Michael says.

Detective Broadus checks his notepad. "Michael?"

"Yes."

He looks at me. "And you're Nicki Hill?"

"Yes sir."

He stares at me like he's been in prison and I'm the first woman he's seen since getting released. And when he says, "Michael, stay put. Nicki, come with me," my stomach drops. I look at Michael, hoping he'll intervene, or at least accompany me, but his eyes are tracking Alison and Jessie, who are heading toward him with blankets around their shoulders and a paramedic in tow. What strikes me most about the Thorne women tonight is their curious facial expressions. While clearly distraught, they also seem...*embarrassed*. I spin around, leaving Detective Broadus behind, and rush to their sides, hug them, and tell them how sorry I am. By then Michael's hugging Jessie, waiting to console his mom, and I feel like an outsider. From behind me Broadus says, "Miss Hill? We need to talk. *Now*."

He leads me fifty yards away from the others and stops beside what I assume is his car. Then he gives me a no-nonsense look and says, "How would you describe your relationship with David Thorne?"

I stare at Broadus a minute, trying to read his thoughts. Then say, "We were cordial."

"*Cordial?*"

"Yes sir. I mean, he and Alison—Mrs. Thorne—have been like parents to me."

"Were you sleeping with him?"

"*Excuse* me?"

"It's a simple question, Miss Hill. What I'm asking, were you fucking him?"

"*What? Are you serious?*"

"Yes or no, please. But do yourself a favor: don't lie. Because we'll know the truth soon enough, and if you're lying, it'll come back to bite you."

"Whoa. Are you for real right now?"

"This is as real as it gets, sweetheart. Got an answer for me?"

I feel like I just walked into the middle of a foreign movie with no subtitles. This detective asks about my relationship, and I tell him David's been like a father to me, and his first question is, have I been *fucking* him? That's sick. I mean, has he been fucking *his* parents?

I tell Broadus exactly what I'm thinking: "This is crazy."

"I agree," he says. "But answer the question. And do so with total honesty."

Chapter 3

8:22 p.m.

I'VE SEEN ENOUGH murder mysteries on TV to know anything I say can be used against me, so I take a few seconds to compose my thoughts before answering. Then I stand straight and tall, look him in the eye and say, "David was my fiancé's father. I never had an affair with him, nor would I. My 'relationship' with him, as you call it, was nonexistent, outside of a few family dinners and outings."

"You've never met him away from the family?"

"What do you mean?"

"Just the two of you?"

I nearly say no, but catch myself. "We had coffee once."

"When was that?"

"About three months ago."

"Any particular reason?"

"Michael and I had recently broken up and the Thornes wanted me to reconsider. I met with each of them one-on-one: Alison, Jessie, and David."

"And where did this meeting with David take place?"

"Starbucks."

"Which one?"

I tell him, then ask, "What's this about?"

"*Really*, Miss Hill? The man *died* today. We're investigating it."

"We were told he hanged himself."

He stares at me, saying nothing, so I ask, "Is that not what happened?"

"How about I ask the questions?"

I shrug.

He says, "Where else had you met Mr. Thorne?"

"Like I said: family get-togethers."

"Did you ever meet him in private? Just the two of you?"

"No. Just..."

"Yes?"

"That time at Starbucks."

"You're sure about that?"

"Yes. Are we done here?"

"Almost."

He removes his phone from his pants pocket, searches for something, finds it, and tilts the screen so I can see it. "Wait," he says. "Let me adjust the brightness." After doing so he says, "We found this photo on David's phone. Can you explain it to me?"

"Of course. That's me, taking a selfie with Mr. Thorne."

"And where were you at the time?"

"In a restaurant, with his family."

He frowns, so I explain: "It was Christmas weekend. Look: you can see Jessie in the background."

He stares at the photo like it's his wife with another guy. Finally, I ask: "Why are you grilling me about this?"

"You think I'm *grilling* you? Believe me, if I ever start *grilling* you, you'll know it."

"I know it already. You keep accusing me of having an affair with my fiancé's father even after I've denied it. You're making it sound like an innocent photo is *murder* evidence. Am I a murder suspect?"

"Should you be?"

I roll my eyes. "Of course not. I'm 112 pounds with clothes on. How could I possibly hang a 220-pound man?"

"You know his exact weight?"

"Everyone does. He was obsessed with his weight. Talked about it all the time." When Broadus says nothing I ask, "Can I go now?"

"Suit yourself."

I turn away, but before I take the first step he says, "One last thing."

I sigh, then turn to face him.

"What did you do to make David so angry?"

"Excuse me?"

"As I said, the photo I showed you came from his phone. But he kept a printed copy in a frame."

"So?"

"Why would he keep a framed photo of the two of you?"

"He was being polite."

"What do you mean?"

"After I took the photo I emailed him a copy. Later on I printed it, put it in a frame, and sent it with a message thanking him for including me at their family event."

"You're saying he felt obligated to keep it?"

"That's my guess."

"And did you take a selfie with Alison as well?"

"I wanted to, but she hates selfies. So no. But I *did* send her a gift and thank you note for making me feel so welcome at Christmas."

"What was the gift?"

"Laser-cut thank you notes."

He writes it down in his pad and stares at it while I wait for him to speak. When he doesn't, I ask, "Why are you making such a big deal out of my stupid selfie picture?"

"We found it on the floor, across the room from his body."

"I don't understand."

"Neither do we. But it appears the last thing David Thorne did before hanging himself was throw your selfie across the room so hard it smashed the frame and put a dent the wall. Any idea why he might do that?"

"No. But..."

"Yes?"

"At least I understand why you're asking these crazy questions."

"Have you heard the circumstances concerning the body? How he was found?"

"I only heard he hanged himself."

I look at him for an explanation, but all he says is, "I'm sure the others will tell you."

I walk back to where Michael and his family had been, but Jessie's the only one there. She's as distraught as I'd expect, which makes me wonder why Alison and Michael aren't comforting her.

"Where's your mom?"

"She and Michael are talking. They told me to wait for you, and said when you were done with the detective maybe we could hang together. Can we?"

I cringe at her use of the word *hang*, and wait to see if she realizes what she said. But she doesn't, so I say: "Of course. Want to walk a bit?"

She does, so we head down the long driveway and turn right at the road and continue till we reach the end of their fence line. Then I ask, "What's your mom talking to Michael about?"

"I'm not sure, but they're definitely up to something."

"Like what?"

15

"I think they're talking about the insurance...and about *you*."

"*Me?* Why?"

"I don't know. Something about what the detectives were asking."

"I see. Is there anything *you* want to ask me?"

"No, but...I might want to talk to you about something else." She hastens to add, "But I'm not ready yet."

"That's fine. Whenever you're ready, just let me know."

"Thanks, Nicki."

Two local news vans race past us with their flashers on. We watch them drive right up to the edge of the Thorne's driveway, and park.

"We'd better head back," I say.

Jessie agrees, and by the time we get there the news crews are standing in the front yard, shooting video footage.

"Assholes!" I say. "Act like we're gawkers, not family members."

"How do gawkers act?"

"I don't know, actually."

Despite the seriousness of the occasion, she giggles. As we walk past the reporters she calls out, "Don't film us. We're not part of the family. We're just gawkers."

When we find Michael and Alison he says "The police finally let us go inside, so Mom packed some things so you guys can stay with us at a hotel for the night."

"Preferably one that's at least ten miles away," Alison says. "We'll try to get some sleep and deal with all this in the morning."

"What about Daddy?" Jessie says.

Alison looks at Michael. He says, "The coroner's office has assumed temporary custody of his body till they decide whether or not to hold an official inquest."

"What's that?"

"An official meeting where they try to establish the manner of death. In other words, was it a suicide, a homicide, or an accident?"

"We should be there."

"There's nothing we can do," Alison says. "But they told us we could see him late tomorrow or anytime Friday. In the meantime, I've packed what you need for the night. We should get whatever sleep we can, because tomorrow's going to be awful."

Michael and I decide on the Griffin Gate Marriott and he drives the four of us there. We book a room for Alison and Jessie, and one for ourselves, and help them settle in. Since no one feels like going to the hotel restaurant, Michael orders room service for us, and when it arrives we eat in stony silence. After dinner he and I go to our room and he says, "Dad was our rock. I can't believe he's gone." He sits on the bed and suddenly bursts into tears. I do what I can to comfort him and before I know it he's climbing all over me, pulling off my clothes, pinning me beneath him, forcing me to...I'm shocked and stunned and...I'm serious: he's sexually *assaulting* me! I want no part of it, but...I lie there and bite my lip and absorb each angry thrust until he finally collapses on top of me, exhausted and spent.

Dazed, and in considerable pain, I slide out from under him and trudge on unsteady legs to the bathroom and lock the door. My thighs are shaking so violently I have to lean my elbows on the sink in order to gradually work myself down onto the toilet. Now, sitting here, I expect to feel some measure of relief, but for whatever reason the act of sitting enhances the pain. I reach up and grab the large towel from the towel rod and press it into my face and mouth to keep my crying as silent as possible, then wonder why I even *care* about being quiet. I should march in there and pummel him with my fists! I'm hurt, humiliated, and thoroughly disillusioned by the man who—just hours ago—professed his undying love in a coffee shop over a fucking latte.

I want to scream at him for—is it too much to say? That he basically *raped* me?

No. It wasn't a 'basically' sort of thing. He *absolutely* raped me. My insides are on fire! I take a deep breath and pee, and it stings like crazy. I look down, expecting blood in the toilet, but thankfully there's none. But when I wipe there's some spotting. Not much, and not from the pee, but he obviously tore me up enough to create some small fissures.

I look through the bag I stuffed with everything I might need for a multi-day trip and find an old pill box with two leftover Percocets. I take one for the pain, and tell myself not to overreact. Of course he wasn't in his right mind. He just lost his father, and it wasn't a sudden death, it was suicide, and obviously that's a million times harder to process.

I get all that.

But it still doesn't give him a free pass to brutalize me. Because if I'm supposed to rationalize what he did and accept it under the heading of 'he just lost his father', then what if I hadn't been here tonight? Would he have had the right to go down to the lobby bar and rape some other poor woman?

No. And nor do I believe he would have done that.

So yes, I'm taking it personally. And I'll never be able to view him the same way again, because what does it say about a man whose first response to tragedy is physically assaulting his fiancée?

The more I think about it, the angrier I get. He offered no apology, no explanation, and when I gasped in pain he continued without the slightest hesitation.

I finish crying, get to my feet, wash the tears from my face, brush my teeth...and try to decide what to do next. Because I'm sure as shit not going to climb back in his bed. I will *not* accept his next assault passively.

I put my ear to the door and listen.

He's snoring. That should make me feel grateful, but it doesn't.

It pisses me off.

How can he be so oblivious to my situation? I think about it a minute, then tell myself it doesn't matter. It's time to make a decision. Should I stay in here all night, climb in the tub, try to fall asleep?

No.

Because if he needs to pee in the middle of the night I'll have to let him in and we'll spend the next hour talking about what happened. And I truly don't want to talk about it. Not now, not ever. So what's left? Should I call Alison and see if she'll let me stay with her and Jess? Should I run away? *What should I do?*

My inner voice provides the answer: *David's dead. All your plans have gone to shit. Call the police, Nicki. Report the rape.*

Chapter 4

11:20 p.m.

I UNLOCK THE bathroom door, pad quietly across the room, retrieve my phone from the nightstand, take it back to the bathroom, and wonder if I should dial "O" for the operator, or just 911. I opt for 911, but before I press the first digit I remember something my friend Lexi once told me about rape and the law. Lexi, a gifted law student, said: "Legally, there's a fine line between rape and rough sex that comes down to a single word: *stop!*" If Lexi happened to be here right now she'd ask, "At any time before or during the attack, did you tell him no? Did you resist his advances or fight him off? Did you tell him to stop?"

In other words, from a legal standpoint, Lexi would say what happened to me tonight was rough sex, not rape. And while I can make this phone call and ruin Michael's life for a day or two, I'm the one that's going to end up looking bad.

In retrospect, should I have told him to stop? Of course. But it all happened so quickly and unexpectedly, and I was so caught up in the emotional aftermath of David's death and how it affected Michael—I was overwhelmed and startled at the same time. My empathy became his consent.

As I stare at my phone, wondering how often these silent assaults might occur in relationships, my screen lights up with an incoming text from Jessie, who wrote: *Can't sleep. Standing outside your door. Still awake?*

I text back: *Be right there*, then exit the bathroom and use the light from my phone to illuminate my suitcase as I dig for clothes. I get dressed and slip out the door.

Chapter 5

Thursday

12:15 a.m.

"HOW'S YOUR MOM holding up?"

"I drugged her," Jessie says, then laughs at my expression and adds, "With her permission, of course! Two sleeping pills, eight ounces of Grey Goose. Trust me, she's totally zonked. And she's gonna need it, since I doubt she'll sleep four hours in the next four days."

Jess and I are on the far side of the lobby, sitting on a luggage bench by the empty bell captain's desk. She's fidgeting, and her eyes are so swollen you'd think she's DeNiro's stunt double in *Raging Bull.* She wants to tell me something, but she's holding back. So I make small talk till she says, "I assume Michael told you about Daddy."

I want to ask "What about him?" but that seems callous.

"It's so *embarrassing!*" she says.

"What is?"

She looks at me incredulously. "Michael didn't *tell* you?"

"He's said nothing. I don't even know if your dad left a note."

"He didn't."

I close my eyes and try to keep my relief from showing. But in my mind, I'm jumping up and down, doing a cheer. "What's embarrassing?"

She says nothing, just shakes her head.

"Jessie?"

She says, "I'll tell you, but you can't look at me while I say it."

"Okay," I say, thinking *What the fuck?* I turn my head and fix my gaze on the lonely desk clerk reading a paperback on the opposite side of the lobby.

"Nicki?"

"Yeah?"

"Don't look at me till after I've said everything, okay?"

"Okay."

She takes a deep breath, then says, "I'm the one who found the body."

"*Omigod*, Jess!" I say, and nearly turn to comfort her, but she says, "Daddy would be horrified to know that. He thought I was playing golf at the club, but it was so cold I backed out and called Uber to get a ride home."

I understand why she'd be shocked, horrified, or even physically sick to come home and find her dad swinging from a rope. But those weren't the words she used. She said she was *embarrassed*, and I'd like to know why.

And then, without my asking, she tells me.

Chapter 6

12:30 a.m.

"HE WAS NAKED."

I know I promised not to look at Jessie's face, but it's not easy. Nor can I come up with a proper response. So I wait till she says, "Completely naked. And that's not the worst part..." her words trail off and she starts huffing to keep from crying, but it doesn't work and she suddenly hugs me and starts sobbing. I comfort her as best I can and now I'm looking into her eyes and she does the last possible thing I expect: she kisses me.

On the lips.

Sensually.

And now I'm thinking, *What the fuck is it with this family's reaction to grief? What's next? Is Alison gonna wake up and come at me with a strapon?*

Jessie recoils in horror and says, "Omigod! I don't know why I did that!"

"It's okay."

"No, seriously, I—I don't know what happened just now. I've never—"

I wave her off. "It's okay. You're under a lot of stress. It's nothing. Forget it."

She nods, but says nothing, and I give her time to think about what to say next. Obviously, I want to hear about David's suicide, but she says, "I'm glad that happened just now."

I look at her.

"Don't laugh," she says, "but I've obsessed over you for months. I always looked forward to seeing you. Especially the times you came into my room to talk."

"I've always enjoyed those talks."

"It showed. You really listened to what I had to say. You're the first—and only—person in the world who really understands me."

Not knowing what else to say, I come up with: "There's nothing I'd rather do than be with you, Jess. You're amazing. I was so pleased you always made time for me."

She blushes. "I really shouldn't say this, but...I think about you all the time. I honestly think I'm gay. At least where you're concerned."

"Um..."

She laughs. "Omigod, your face! You're so cute right now! And I'm like, 'Omigod Jessie, shut up! She'll think you're a stalker! She'll never speak to you again.' But the floodgates are open, Nicki, and I can't stop. I know I'm babbling, and don't know where all this is coming from. I can't believe I'm telling you all this. I'm sure it's the vodka I sneaked. It's the vodka, right? Please don't hate me, Nicki. I'd just die if you do."

I put my hand on her cheek and say, "I could never hate you, Jess."

"Even after hearing me say I love you and how I constantly fantasize about us being together sexually?"

I laugh. "Actually, you didn't say those things till just now."

"I *didn't?* Oh, *God!* I think I've gone stark raving mad. I mean, holy shit, you're going to marry my *brother!* I'm like the worst person *ever!*"

I remove my hand from her cheek and say, "Relax. You've been very open with me just now, and whether it was due to the vodka or because of everything that's happened today I think you were incredibly brave to tell me how you feel."

I notice she's looking at me with elevated interest and wide, hopeful eyes, so I add: "I know you want me to respond, but you've had these thoughts for a while, and I'm hearing them for the first time. I honestly had no idea you felt this way, and it's a lot for me to process. But can I tell you something?"

"You can tell me anything, Nicki."

I don't know if her stunning revelation amounts to a game-changer, but I don't want to take it off the table. Until six o'clock last night I had the perfect plan, then David killed himself, and now his daughter has the hots for me. I mean, who'd believe I'd wind up being loved and lusted for by *both* Thorne kids? It's an ego boost for sure, but since Jessie's looking at me with soulful eyes I need to decide how best to respond. Is it right to put her in the middle of this?

Absolutely not. But *would* I?

These are the tough questions you have to wrestle with when you're in the revenge business. David's death was a complete surprise and a major setback from which I'll have to regroup. Do I really want to get romantically involved with his daughter? I really like Jessie, and she's completely innocent in all this. I'd truly hate to exploit her. That said, it can't hurt to have her in my corner during this transition phase.

"Tell me what you're thinking," she says. "I'm dying to know."

I look into her eyes. "This is just a first impression, okay?"

She nods.

"And a confession." Sternly, I say: "You can't repeat this to anyone."

"I won't. I swear."

"I'll start with the confession: I'm not going to marry Michael."

She gasps. "You're *not*? *Why?*"

"We're not compatible. And more importantly, I don't love him."

She covers her mouth with her hand. "Omigod! Have you *told* him?"

"Not yet."

"He's gonna be *devastated!*"

"I know. I was planning to tell him, then this happened. I still can't believe your Dad—"

She looks down, then back up at me. "You should put it off for at least a week or two."

"You think?"

She nods, then says, "What's the other part you were gonna tell me? About your first impression to what I said?"

"I'm going to be completely honest with you, but if this comes out wrong, please give me another chance to say it better."

"I'll give you all the chances you want."

"Good. So like I said, your words caught me by surprise, but... when you kissed me, it...really moved me."

"It *did?*"

"More than you could imagine. It's like you woke up something inside me I never knew was there, and..." I take a moment to savor the look in her eyes, because you hardly ever get to see this degree of hope and yearning on a person's face. Finally I say, "I think if I could get past the *technical* issues..."

"Like what?"

"Our age difference."

"Six years? That's not so much."

It really is. She's fifteen, I'm twenty-three. She only *thinks* I'm twenty-one. But there's more: "You're a minor."

"Newsflash Nicki: age of consent is sixteen! I'm only weeks away."

"How many, to be exact?"

"Six."

I smile. "Interesting you've already checked on Kentucky's consent laws, but now that I think about it, I wonder if it applies to females. Do you know?"

She shakes her head no, then flashes a sly smile and says, "I'm willing to take a chance it only applies to penetration."

I'll *bet* she is! But she's not the one who'll be wearing prison stripes for five years. Then again, who knows what the hell the law is, since cops and prosecutors pick and choose which ones to enforce, and how and when to do so. For example, I know from my foster home experience if an underage girl and boy have sex they may or may not prosecute, but if they do, they'll only prosecute the boy. So the law is whatever their whim is on any given day.

Jessie slides one of her legs toward me till it makes contact with mine. Her cutoffs are revealing a lot of thigh, so I trace my fingers lightly over her skin while saying, "This is major, Jess. I've never been with a woman before."

"God I *love* you!" she coos. "See? That's what I'm talking about, Nicki."

"What?"

"You don't even realize what you said. And that's what makes you so amazing!"

"Thanks. But I have no idea what you're talking about."

"You said you've never been with a woman."

"I haven't."

She smiles. "What you *didn't* say is you've never been with a *girl* before. After pointing out I'm technically a minor, you referred to me as a woman."

"Well, that's how I see you."

She grins.

Figuring this is as good a time as any to get back on subject, I dive right in: "You said you found your father naked, but that wasn't the worst part. What was?"

And she says:

Chapter 7

12:50 a.m.

"HE WAS HOLDING his penis."

"Excuse me?"

"He had a hard on."

"Oh, Jess!"

"It's...I mean—the police called it auto-something."

"Had he been watching porn?"

She does a double-take. "How did you *know?*"

"Autoerotic asphyxiation."

"That's it. But what does it *mean?* Was Daddy a pervert?"

"Of course not."

"Mom says he was. Michael said it too."

"Because of *this?*"

"Uh huh."

"Had he ever done anything else?"

"I don't know. They won't say."

"Were they shocked?"

"Totally!"

"Then it's probably his first time. And your mom's probably pissed at him for taking his life. But that doesn't mean he was a pervert. I'm certain he wasn't."

"Then why would he...I mean, Mom and Michael won't even *talk* to me about it."

"Don't be too harsh on them. They're trying to protect you because—"

"They still think of me as a child."

"Exactly. But I don't see you that way. So if you really want to hear about it, I'm glad to give you my take. Then again, it's your dad we're talking about, so if you're not comfortable, just tell me and I won't say another word."

"It's okay. I want to know what happened."

"It's pretty simple, really. Your dad was jerking off, nothing more."

"Well, it was clearly a lot more."

"Right. Of course it was. What I meant was, autoerotic asphyxiation is jerking off while cutting off oxygen to the brain."

"By hanging himself?"

"It's more common than you think. A lot of famous people do it."

"Like who?"

"Singers. Celebrities. Movie stars."

"Why?"

"For the rush. They tie a noose, stand on a bucket or whatever, and jack off. As the noose tightens, it cuts off the oxygen to the brain, and it's supposed to create some sort of high."

"Like a drug?"

"That's my understanding."

"I don't get it."

"You don't? Have you never masturbated?"

She blushes.

"It's okay. We all do. Even your mom."

"*What?*"

"I guarantee it."

"Eew!"

"Relax. Everyone does it."

"You too?"

"*Especially* me."

She laughs.

"But your dad apparently took it to another level. I don't know all the technical details, but if you're interested I've got an expert right here in my pocket." I pull out my phone, access the search engine, scan the first article that pops up, read it, then translate: "It has to do with the carotid arteries in your neck. When they get compressed, the sudden loss of oxygen to the brain causes something called hypoxia. When combined with an orgasm, it produces a high that's equivalent to cocaine, and just as addictive."

"Wow. You think Daddy was into that?"

"I don't know."

"What else does it say?"

"Just that the people who do it are called gaspers, because they're gasping for breath."

"It's practically suicide."

"I think that's part of the allure. They're gambling they'll be able to loosen the rope before passing out, and they usually do. But when it goes wrong, it's deadly."

I look up to see an icy look pass over her face. She says, "If Mom had been giving it up for Daddy he'd still be alive. Don't you agree, Michael?"

From behind me, Michael snarls, "Don't you *ever* say that again!"

"Were you *spying* on us?" I say, unable to contain the anger in my voice.

"Don't be stupid. I just got here. But I have to admit I was surprised to wake up and see you left the room the one night in my life I needed you most."

"Get used to it," I whisper, looking straight into Jessie's eyes.

"I'm sorry, did you just *say* something?" he says, without trying to hide his bitterness.

Jess comes to my defense: "She only left the room because I asked her to. I couldn't sleep. But it's sure nice to know *you* had no problem sleeping."

"What's *that* supposed to mean?" He grabs my arm and spins me around so I have to look at him. "What did you tell her about me?"

"Leave her alone!" Jess says, jumping to her feet. "What's your *problem*, Michael? She didn't say *anything* about you."

He gives her a long look, then growls, "Party's over. Let's go, Nicki."

"I don't think so," I say.

His eyes are like two smoldering coals. He's livid. Angrier than I've ever seen him, which is a perfect reason not to accompany him back to his fuck den. Not that I needed a perfect reason. I pull away from Michael's grip and look at Jessie. "Got any space in your room for me?"

"Of course," she says. "Michael, stop being a jerk. You were asleep and Nicki was just trying to comfort me."

"Fuck you both," he says, and stomps off.

Jessie says, "Has he ever treated you like this before?"

I shrug. "Like I said, we're not compatible."

"What happened tonight between you guys?"

I bite my lip. "I probably shouldn't tell you."

"You can tell me anything."

"He raped me."

"*What?*"

"He was upset about your dad, and took it out on me. I'm sure he didn't mean it."

"Don't make excuses for him," she snaps. Then softens her voice. "Are you okay?"

"I'm sore, but...yeah. Sadly, I've had worse experiences, though it's been a while."

"You definitely need to bail on the relationship."

"I know."

"Not in a week or two. Right now!"

"I don't want to be cruel."

"Are you *kidding* me?" she says.

"I especially don't want your mom to think I'm abandoning him when he needs me."

"You've got no choice, Nicki. I've never seen that side of him. The look in his eyes was terrifying. You can't trust him."

"I agree."

"Good. Then it's settled," she says. "Thank God!"

She sits beside me, gives my mouth a quick kiss, then leans back to see how I'll respond.

I say, "Can I ask *you* a question?"

"Anything."

"How zonked is your mom?"

Her face brightens. "Let's put it this way: we could use her body for a dance floor!"

"Would it wake her up if I took a shower in your room?"

She takes my hand in hers, flashes that same sly smile I saw earlier and says, "It wouldn't even wake her up if I took a shower *with* you."

I let that comment hang in the air long enough for her to consider the appropriateness of having felony sex in the same hotel room where her mom is sleeping, on the same night her dad committed suicide. Then I say, "Maybe we should test that theory."

"I'd love to!" she says.

Chapter 8

6:15 a.m.

AS THE FIRST woman in the room to open her eyes, I get home field advantage. That means I can lie here and take stock of the situation, get my bearings, hide all evidence of wrong-doing, and generally prevent any potential problems I'd have to solve later. First things first: how do I feel, physically?

Not great. I'm sore as hell. Michael really did a number on me. I take a moment to wonder again why I didn't fight him off. It's almost as if I *wanted* him to hurt me, and...perhaps I did. I'm sure some part of me felt I deserved to be punished for my despicable behavior. For my cold-hearted planning and scheming. For stringing Michael along all these months. For being at least partially responsible for his father's death.

As for Jess, I can't help but notice her hand is cupping my boob, and to my surprise, I like it. I'm on my back, she's on her side, her lips parted, and her mouth just inches from my nostrils. This is worth noting because it doesn't seem possible her breath could be so sweet and pleasant when every morning mine is rancid enough to repel

35

a rabid wolverine. I assume this is a happy byproduct of her age. Speaking of morning breath, while mine is typically horrendous, this morning it's even worse than usual. I slide my tongue across my teeth and swallow, thinking *Why are my lips so swollen? What in God's name is that taste in my mouth? Did I eat someth—*

Oh.

Right.

I look at Jess.

Could I go to jail for that?

Probably.

But if nothing else, we made a memory. And Jess was right: her mom slept through the whole thing. Completely missed her daughter's first orgasm. Because of what Michael did to me we kept the lovemaking mostly about welcoming Jessie to the grownup's table: she kissed me from the waist up and I kissed her from the waist down and we both got what we needed. Having said that, I'm finding myself looking forward to the next time, if there is one.

So she's sleeping and Alison's sleeping, and I'm feeling around under the covers to make sure I'm wearing my T-shirt and panties and...I am.

That being the case, whose Hello Kitty panties are these?

Two guesses.

I lift my head to make sure Alison's still sleeping.

She is.

I need to wake Jessie up, get her hand off my boob, get her panties back on her body before Alison wakes up and discovers how close her daughter and I have grown since her husband's death.

Chapter 9

7:20 a.m.

AFTER LEAVING JESS in her room, I head to mine and try to enter quietly, but apparently Michael set the latch because the door only opens a couple of inches before making a huge racket.

"Michael?"

"What?"

"Can you let me in, please?"

"I thought you wanted to be elsewhere."

I sigh. Is there anything worse than a GMP (Grown Man Pouting)? And while we're on the subject, as I'm standing here in the hall, how about we address his behavior toward *me*: I tried to console him last night and he *assaulted* me. I wanted to take away his pain even as he wanted to inflict pain on me, the woman he supposedly loves and wants to spend the rest of his life with. Then he found me with his sister and became furious that I "abandoned" him (when he needed me most).

Abandoned him?

Who *wouldn't* abandon a rapist after being raped? Only a fool would go back to the scene of the crime, angry as Michael was, after what he'd done. Let's not forget, this is the same guy who claims to worry about my safety and lectures me about how men can't be trusted, and how I'm oblivious to their glances and lewd remarks. He's the one who goes through that whole verbal checklist about what I should and shouldn't do when he's not around. But you know what he left off the list?

Being in a hotel room with *him!*

So now I'm supposed to what, apologize for abandoning him when he needed me most? For not coming back to the room in the wee hours of the morning to be raped a second time?

As it turns out, that's not what he expects. What he wants is answers. Specifically: "Were you fucking my father?"

I roll my eyes in the hallway and again when he finally allows me to enter the room.

"*Were* you?"

"So that's why you raped me last night?"

"*What? Raped* you? Believe me, if I ever decide to rape you, you'll know it."

I wonder why people keep telling me if they decide to do something I'll know it. If the detective ever grills me, I'll know it. If my fiancé ever rapes me, I'll know it. I *do* fucking know it!

"Don't sell yourself short, Michael. I've been raped before, and believe me, you don't have to take a back seat to anyone."

"You think that's funny?"

"Funny's the last word I'd use."

"Fuck you, Nicki! And for your information, my mom told me your whole foster family sob story months ago."

I look at him. "You've got a cruel streak, Michael. Anyone ever tell you that?"

"So do you. By the way, I notice you haven't bothered to answer my question. Were you fucking my father?"

"No. And you *know* it."

"Then why do two police detectives think you were?"

"Because they're morons. They found a stupid picture on the floor and thought, 'The dad must be fucking his son's fiancée!' Well, how nice of them to say. On the other hand, they're seasoned detectives who've seen every type of horror there is, so I doubt *anything's* far-fetched to them. There's a photo on the floor? Could it be the husband and wife were fighting and one of them picked up the thing that was closest—a stupid selfie photo—and threw it across the room in anger? No. Too easy. The photo on the floor means the dad and his future daughter-in-law were having an affair. And why not? They don't know me, they didn't know your dad, so in their eyes it's a possibility. But *you* know me, Michael, and you knew your dad your whole life, so I have to ask, is this what you really think about him? Or is it what you think about me?"

"Nice speech."

"Fuck you, Michael."

"I would, but you'd accuse me of rape."

I show him the angriest look I can muster while saying nothing. Because after last night I really don't know what he's capable of doing.

I lock myself in the bathroom with a clean change of clothes and take another Percocet, then shower, add some color to my face, and open the door to an empty room.

Fine with me.

I text Jessie, who texts back that her mom and Michael are on their way to meet David's insurance agent. That strikes me as odd, so I call her phone. When she answers I ask, "Kind of soon to be filing for the death benefit, don't you think?"

"Actually, the insurance guy called Mom to say how sorry he was."

"How would *he* know so quickly?"

"He's a neighbor."

"Still, it seems kind of cold to meet him this soon."

"Think about it, Nicki."

"What do you mean?"

"It's Mr. Blass. Daddy's insurance agent. Our *neighbor*."

"*Omigod! That's* the guy? Whoa! My head's about to explode!"

"Exactly. So Mom wanted to explain how Daddy died."

"Blass didn't know?"

"Apparently not."

"Where are they meeting?"

"At the house. Michael didn't tell you?"

"We're not talking so much these days. He left while I was in the shower."

"I bet that wasn't as fun as *our* shower."

"You'd win that bet. How come *you* didn't go with them?"

"Mom said to stay put. They didn't want me there."

"Why not?"

"Mom's gonna say Daddy did this auto-sex thing all the time."

"Why?"

"Michael said the insurance pays twice as much for an accident than it does for suicide."

"Double indemnity?"

"I guess. Can I come to your room?"

"That's fraud, Jess. About the insurance, I mean."

"That's what Mom said. But Michael said there's no proof he didn't do it all the time. It just makes sense he did, especially because of the noose. Plus, I'm sure Mr. Blass will do all he can to help Mom get the money."

"No doubt. But what's the deal about the noose?"

"The detectives said it was a slip knot instead of a hangman's knot, and that's how the auto-sex guys do it. But I can't imagine

Daddy knew anything about tying the kind of knots he'd need to hang himself. You think he bought it somewhere?"

I laugh. "You mean like a suicide store?"

She shakes her head. "Forget I said that. I'm such an idiot sometimes."

"Not to me. You're brilliant, far as I'm concerned. So this whole insurance scam was Michael's idea?"

"Yup. But he didn't have to twist Mom's arm. She's in it 100%."

"Did they ask *you* to lie?"

"Nope. I'm just a child, remember? I'm not supposed to know anything."

"You're no child."

"Not after last night," she giggles. "Can I come over?"

I pause. "How about we meet downstairs for breakfast? I'm starving. Aren't you?"

"I guess. Are you blowing me off?"

"No, of course not."

"Are you sure? Because I had a really great time last night."

"Me too."

"Then why can't we..."

"Order room service?"

"Uh huh."

"I'm twenty-three."

"What?"

"I'm twenty-three years old."

"No you're not. You're twenty-one, same as Michael."

"I lied about my age."

"No shit? Why?"

"I don't know. The night I met him he asked me, and it just came out. Then, once we started dating, I just...never corrected it."

"He's never seen your driver's license?"

"If he did, he never checked the date."

"What made you tell *me* just now?"

"I really like you. I thought you should know."

"Twenty-three?"

"Yup."

"That's really sweet, Grandma," she says, then laughs hysterically.

When she's done I ask, "So it's not a problem? The age difference?"

"No. And don't worry: I'll keep your secret."

"Thanks."

"We've all got secrets, Nicki."

"Tell me one of yours."

She says, "Here's one I've been saving. Ready?"

"Let's hear it."

"I'm adopted."

Chapter 10

8:15 a.m.

"WHAT DO YOU *mean* you're adopted? Who told you *that?*"

"Michael. And then I confronted Mom and Daddy and they confirmed it."

"When did this happen?"

"Years ago, when I was ten. I was being a brat and Michael got pissed and said I wasn't his real sister."

"What a *bastard*! Has he always been like that?"

"Who cares? You're still gonna leave him, right?"

"Absolutely. And soon."

"Good. Can I come over now?"

"Yes. And hurry!"

Of course I knew Jess was adopted. It didn't require much due diligence to discover *that* tidbit. But I had no idea *she* knew, and wonder why she never mentioned it in any of the heart-to-hearts we've shared. As I wait for her to tap on my door I rush through the room, tidying up, picking up stray clothes, pulling the sheets tight to remove the wrinkles, fluffing the pillows. I find my heart racing at the notion

Jess finds me desirable, and though I've never been with a woman before (Oh God, should I say *girl?*) —I always wanted to try. But I never *dreamed* I'd enjoy it as much as I did last night.

Moments later, we're in the bed naked. "I wish you weren't so sore," she says.

"What did you have in mind?"

"Returning the favor."

"In that case, I'm fine."

"You sure?"

"Never better! Not to mention I've taken two pain pills since...it happened."

"I don't want to hurt you."

"At this point it would hurt more if you didn't."

She digs in, and we're both right: it hurts, but it's worth it. Afterward, I order room service and we get dressed while waiting for our food to arrive. As we eat, I ask, "How was your mom this morning?"

"Loopy. She got up, brushed her teeth, put her skirt on backwards and didn't even know. Good thing I was there to tell her."

"Did she happen to mention the detectives accused me of having an affair with your dad?"

She laughs. "Wait, are you being *serious?*"

I nod.

"Why on earth would they think *that?*"

"You know that selfie I took with him the day after Christmas?"

Her face falls. "Oh shit. I'm sorry, Nicki."

"For what?"

"I was hoping you wouldn't find out about that. I wanted to get it fixed."

"What happened?"

"When I walked in and saw Daddy's body I went crazy. I ran for the door and knocked the photo off the table and it broke."

"The detectives said they found it on the opposite side of the room, and that it had been thrown so hard it made a dent in the wall."

"Baseboard."

"What?"

"When Mom saw the body and realized he was dead she screamed at him, called him a bastard, and for a minute I thought she was gonna punch him in the ribs. But she changed her mind and kicked the picture frame instead. It didn't have anything to do with your selfie. She was just mad at Daddy, and it was there." She pauses. "What does that have to do with them thinking you had an affair with Daddy?"

"They saw the broken picture of me and him and wondered if maybe he broke it out of anger. And if so, then maybe we had an affair, and I threatened to tell your mom, and that's why he killed himself."

"They said all that?"

"Everything except the part about telling your mom. I added that, but I think it's what they were implying."

She shakes her head. "That's crazy."

"I said the exact same thing."

Fifteen seconds pass with no response from Jess, so I say, "I didn't have an affair with your dad. You know that, right?"

"You swear?"

"On my life."

She studies my face. Then says, "I believe you. I mean, it's not like you even *live* here. When would you have the time?"

"There are better reasons than *that*! Aside from the fact he was nearly twice my age, I would never *do* that."

"Of course not."

We're quiet till she says, "And just so you know, I never suspected you!"

"Of what?"

"I mean, toward the end I thought he might be having an affair because Mom accused him of it. I just never knew who the woman was. Do you?"

"How the fuck would *I* know?"

She laughs. "Nicki?"

"Yeah?"

"Is it too soon to tell you I love you?"

"Not if it's true."

"It's true."

"I love you, too, Jess."

And just like that, we're officially a couple.

Well, not *officially*.

But within seconds we're officially naked again.

Chapter 11

10:30 a.m.

THE DOOR SUDDENLY opens!

I lift my head and gasp, fearing the worst. But thank God it's the maid, not Michael and Alison, who would certainly be surprised to find us in bed, in this particular position, naked. The maid—bless her heart—went straight to the bathroom, pretending not to see us, which Jess, being young, thinks is hilarious.

"We've got to be more careful!" I scold. "What if it had been your brother?"

"My brother Michael would handle it a lot better than your fiancé Michael."

"Not funny, Jess. Seriously. It could have been your mom."
"So?"
"Are you prepared for them to know what we've done?"
She looks at me. "Aren't you?"
"No. Not yet, I mean."
"Why not?"
"Think about it."

"The timing? Sooner or later they'll have to face the fact we're in love."

"Let's make it later."

"Why? Because you're already having second thoughts?"

I sigh. "A little while ago, in the moment, you said you loved me and I said I loved you too. I don't regret saying that, because I've always had feelings for you as a friend. This part is obviously new to me, and I'm really enjoying it. I'm eager to explore where it could go, and have no reason to believe it wouldn't be perfect, but I guess what I'm saying—"

"You're not really in love with me."

"That's not what I'm saying at all! Let me try again: emotions are already running high with Michael and me. If he found out about us it would put him over the top. Why are you shaking your head?"

"Because you're making it sound like your biggest fear is Michael's state of mind, and that's simply not true. You're afraid they're gonna find out we've been having sex and they're gonna do the math and realize you're an adult and I'm a minor and...what's wrong?"

"Are you *threatening* me?"

"*What?* Of *course* not! How can you even *think* that?

Looking into her face I see nothing but innocence. But now I find myself wondering how well I really know her. Despite the fact she wanted me first, the power in our relationship has shifted dramatically: she literally has the power to destroy me. So I say, "Did you mean it earlier when you said you love me?"

"You know I did, Nicki. And the reason you know is because after thinking about it you can look back and see I've loved you for months. From the day we met I opened up to you and told you things about me that no one else knows. The real question is where are *you* in this relationship?"

"I already told you. I love you too."

"Yes. You *did* say that."

"You don't believe me?"

"It's certainly what I wanted to hear. But now that I think about it, your pronouncement came awfully quick."

"I wouldn't mislead you, Jess."

After a moment of silence, she says: "Prove it."

"Prove I *love* you? How?"

"Tell Mom."

"When?"

"Today."

I take a deep breath. "Okay."

She does a double-take. "You will?"

"Yes. If you'll promise to say we've only kissed, and that we've decided to wait till you're sixteen before exploring anything sexual. Can you do that?"

She feigns shock. "You want me to *lie* for you?"

I laugh. "We wouldn't see much of each other if I'm in prison."

"You wouldn't go to prison. It'd be different if you were a 23-year-old guy, but you're not. We're girls. It's totally different."

"You might be right, but I'd hate to bet my future on it. Can we just lie about that one part?"

"On one condition."

"What's that?"

"We get to keep having sex."

"Fine with me, but after today your mom will be watching you like a hawk. Not to mention she's gonna keep us separated as long as you're under her roof."

She frowns. "I hadn't thought about that."

"Well, it's something we ought to consider."

She thinks a moment, then says, "All right."

"All right what?"

"I still want her to know. Today. And Michael, too."

"You're sure?"

She nods. "I want them to hear you say you're leaving Michael, and that you love me."

"And what will you say?"

"I'll tell them I love you and when I'm sixteen I'm going to move in with you...if you'd like that."

"I'd love it, except I'm pretty sure you have to be eighteen to live with me against your Mom's wishes."

"Let's look into it. But either way, I want them to know today."

"Fine. You want to be there when I tell them?"

"Of course."

"Are you gonna back me up about the sex part?"

She pauses. "I'm not sure yet."

"When will you know?"

"Is it a condition for telling them?"

"No."

"Then it doesn't matter, does it?"

"I guess not."

She cocks her head. "You're really gonna tell them? You swear to God?"

"Yes."

She stares at me. "You're bluffing your ass off!"

"You'll see I'm not."

"I guess we'll both see, soon enough."

A voice says, "It's right decision."

We look up and see the maid standing ten feet away. How long she's been there is anyone's guess, but certainly long enough to offer her unsolicited opinion. "Always best to tell truth," she says. Then adds, "Nice tits, both. Should I make bed now or come back?"

Chapter 12

11:45 a.m.

WE GET DRESSED, leave the room, walk around the lobby and mezzanine while talking about our feelings. Then Jess says, "I've been acting inappropriately since Daddy died."

"Not true. I saw you shortly after it happened. You were grief-stricken."

"I know, but since then."

"Since then you've been trying to block it out, and that gave you the strength to tell me how you feel about me. It provided a welcome distraction for your stress."

"Thanks, Doctor Hill. How much do I owe you for the consultation?"

"One kiss."

She says, "You're nice to phrase it that way, but we both know everything you just said is total bullshit. I've been selfish, thinking only of myself and what I want. I had a reason for it, but sometimes it feels like I'm spitting on Daddy's memory."

"I'm sure your dad wouldn't want you to dwell on his death. He'd want you to be happy."

"I hope so. But like I said, I had a reason for doing this now. Can I tell you why?"

"Please do."

"When you asked if I knew the detectives were talking about you and Daddy having an affair I acted surprised, but they said that to me and Mom yesterday before you got to the house. Of course I stuck up for you, but I didn't like what they said about you and Daddy, and I didn't like what Mom and Michael have been saying about you, either."

"They talk about me?"

"All the time. And not in a good way."

"I thought your mom loved me."

"She did, till you went back to Michael the last time. Since then he's had a lot to say, and she's been listening. And when the detectives started asking all those questions I could tell Mom was never going to invite you back."

"That's why you wanted to meet last night?"

"I figured it was the only chance I'd ever have to tell you how I feel."

"Wow. That was pretty damn brave."

"I know, right? I mean, I didn't think you'd *laugh* at me, because we've always been so close. And in the back of my mind I had the smallest hope you might be flattered, or possibly interested, because sometimes when we talked I had the feeling you were looking at me with more than friendship eyes."

"I'm sure I was!"

She smiles. "I know that now. But I kept telling myself I was imagining that part. But when you told me you were going to leave Michael, I put it all out there. I've wanted you, like, forever, and I couldn't bear the thought of never seeing you again."

"You're definitely going to see me again."

We walk silently a few minutes till she says, "You know what really surprises me? You haven't said a word about backing out of telling them we're a couple. That's got to be really hard for you to do."

"I'm glad you understand that."

"Want to do a practice run?"

"You mean right now?"

"Uh huh."

"Fine. How's this: Alison, I know you just lost your husband yesterday, and Michael, you and Jessie lost your dad. And even though David's not yet in the ground, I think today should be all about me, not you, so here's the scoop: I've fallen in love with Jessie, and she loves me. By the way, Michael, I'm not going to marry you. Alison? I want you to know Jess and I haven't had sex yet—*wink, wink!* —but we fully intend to explore the sexual component of our relationship as soon as she turns sixteen. Why am I telling you this today? Well, Jess asked me to, in order to prove my love. How's that?"

She laughs. "Shitty. Let's lose the part about today being all about you, and the 'here's the scoop' part. And the part about how it was my idea to tell them. I want it to come from you."

"You know I was being sarcastic, right?"

"Of course. But still. Want to try again?"

"Not really."

"Fine."

"Fine."

We walk in moody silence for about five minutes before her phone rings. It's Alison, saying they're on their way back to the hotel. Jessie startles me by saying: "Mom? When you guys get here, can you meet us in the lobby? Nicki has something important to tell you."

Those few words uttered so casually into her phone tell me Jess actually expects me to tell her mom and brother we're having an affair! Until this very moment I thought she was just testing me, waiting to see if I'd back down. I never believed she really *meant* it. Not today, at least, and not anytime soon. Now that I know she's serious, I can't fathom her reasons. It's worse than coldhearted, it's downright cruel. And now I'm thinking: *what if she's punishing them, somehow? What if she decides at the last moment not to back me up on the sexual part? What if she tells them everything we've done since last night? What if they call the police?*

Jess hangs up, checks the time, flashes a big grin. "All this time you thought I was kidding, but I wasn't."

I think about denying it, acting cool, like it's no big deal, but she knows better.

"It's best this way," she says.

Chapter 13

12:00 Noon

WE'RE IN THE lobby, occupying the furniture—a couch and two chairs—that probably gets the least use due to its distance from the front desk and the glare from the giant window directly behind it. Speaking of glares, Michael's making no secret how he feels about me at the moment: he's throwing a full-scale pout. But after I tell him I'm leaving him for Jess I guarantee he'll do a 180 and beg me to reconsider. Not because I'm such an amazing catch, but because that's what he does. Michael's cycle of abuse hits five progressions: first, he gets furious. Second, he treats me like shit. Third, I threaten to leave. Fourth, he begs me to stay. Fifth, I agree, and he's wonderful for a few days or weeks...then he gets furious.

"Is this about the insurance?" Michael says, practically spitting the words at me.

"No."

"Really?" He gives Jess a dirty look. "Because I know my big-mouth sister told you about the meeting with Blass."

"Who's Blass?"

"The insurance guy."

Jess says, "This has nothing to do with your little insurance scam. However—"

Alison fixes a cold, steady look on her adopted daughter.

"—Nicki has some information that can make it work. Nicki? Tell them."

Michael and Alison look at me, but I have no idea what she's talking about, so I look at Jessie and say, "Perhaps *you* should tell them."

"Okay, but they probably won't listen, since they think I'm just a stupid kid, and certainly unworthy of helping the family collect on a double indemnity claim."

Alison says, "I'm sorry I've given you that impression, Jessie. I only wanted to protect you and save you the embarrassment. The whole situation is beyond disgusting, and I'm sure you had no idea Daddy's been doing this all along."

Jess says, "Can you *prove* he was?"

Michael says, "Mom's known about it for months. She already told Mr. Blass."

"Except that she's the wife, and has a lot to gain by lying, correct? Where's her proof?"

"Like Mr. Blass says, the proof is in the slip knot. It wasn't a hangman's noose, like the kind people use to kill themselves. Plus, Dad had a cloth around his neck. According to Mr. Blass, that's the strongest evidence of accidental death."

"Sounds like Mr. Blass is working for us instead of the insurance company."

"He's just pointing out the facts. He says that people who...do what Dad did...use a cloth to prevent leaving rope burns around their necks. If Dad was going to kill himself, why would he worry about rope burns?"

"That's all you've got?"

Michael curls his angry lips into a smile. "Mom *saw* him doing it, Jess. And fortunately for us, she came crying to me about it months ago."

Jess frowns. "No one's gonna believe it. No mother would tell her son that her husband's been whacking off with a noose around his neck."

Alison says, "*Shut up*, Jessie! I'm sick of your filthy mouth. This is your *father* we're talking about. Do you understand he's *dead?* Have some respect."

Jess bristles, but keeps quiet.

Alison takes a moment to calm down, then says, "What were you saying about Nicki having some information?"

"I thought you wanted me to shut up."

Alison sighs.

Jess says, "Since you and Michael are beneficiaries, the insurance company will doubt anything you say to them. But Nicki's not in the will, so whatever she says will carry a lot of weight."

Like a snake shedding its skin, Michael's face slowly releases its anger. He's staring at me with great interest as Jess says, "You remember last March when Nicki and Michael spent the night and Nicki agreed to help me with my music project? I had to make a harp, and asked Nicki to get the tool box from Daddy's closet." Jess looks at me and says, "Tell them what you found."

I have no idea what she wants me to say, but as we catch each other's eyes I find myself exhilarated by the trust she's placing in me to be creative, and more than that, I feel like a part of something I've never experienced before. Like what I assume happens when girls with normal childhoods have slumber parties and tell stories where one girl starts it off and each girl adds to it and tries to keep the story going. Knowing full well I should say nothing, I surprise myself and everyone around me by announcing: "David was sitting on the floor, with a rope around his neck."

Alison's eyes grow huge. "Are you *sure*?"

"Positive."

"When was this?"

"Last March."

"Did David see you?"

I nod.

"What did he *say*?"

"He laughed and said, 'Don't be alarmed, I'm just making a Halloween prop.'"

"In *March*?"

I nod.

"And you never mentioned it?"

"She did," Jessie says. "She told *me*."

"When?"

"That night. And I asked Daddy about it."

Michael's jaw drops. "What did he say?"

"Same thing. He was planning to go all out for Halloween this year, and was starting early."

Alison frowns. "That's ridiculous."

Jessie says, "Tell them about the panties."

I look at her with genuine shock. "I-I'd rather not," I say.

"Please, Nicki," Alison says. "Whatever it is, it's okay."

So I say: "He had a pair of women's panties on the floor by the rope."

"Mine?"

"Nicki's," Jessie says.

"What the *fuck*?" Michael says. "My dad stole your panties and you didn't bother to *tell* me?"

"How *could* she?" Jess says. "You would have gone crazy."

"Damn right I would've."

Alison says, "Calm down, Michael. That's quite a story, Nicki, but I can't help wondering why you never seemed the least bit uncomfortable around David all these months. How's that possible?"

Good point. How *is* that possible? I think a moment, then say: "I don't expect you to understand this, but I grew up learning never to speak about the things that bothered me. If something happened to me or someone else, I put it out of my mind and pretended it never happened. It was safer that way."

"I get that," Alison says. "But you've been out of that situation for years. This noose and panty thing supposedly happened last *March?* I don't buy it. You wouldn't be able to look him in the eyes after catching him doing God knows what with your panties."

"*Excuse* me!" Jessie says.

When we look at her she says, "Are you forgetting about *me?* Nicki told *me* about the panties back in March. Have you noticed *me* acting weird around you and Daddy? No? Well that's because Nicki and I had a long talk and agreed not to ever speak of it again. Because she was happy and you and Daddy were happy, and we just decided to pretend it never happened."

Michael says, "Makes sense."

Alison says, "I'm impressed. Tell me about them."

"Excuse me?"

"The panties my husband stole from you. Could you describe them please?"

Jessie says, "Small, thong, black lace, with a white ribbon running through the waistband."

Without taking her eyes off my face, Alison says, "How did you get them back?"

Jessie says, "She didn't. When Daddy and Michael went to play golf the next morning, I went through his things and found them. And kept them."

"Why?"

"I wanted him to know that I knew."

"Knew what?"

"That he had the hots for Nicki."

"That's disgusting!"

"It's true though. Surely *you* knew. Every time Nicki came to visit, Daddy lit up like a Roman candle. He couldn't take his eyes off her."

Alison says nothing.

Jess says, "I was gonna give them back to Nicki next time she visited, but she only came to the house once after that, and that was the day we tried to talk her into going back to Michael. I forgot to give them back. But they're under my mattress, if you care to see them."

Michael says, "Nicki? What was it you wanted to tell us? Jess said it was important."

Chapter 14

I STOP NIBBLING my bottom lip long enough to say: "Michael, I'm sorry to do this today, but after what happened last night, I'm no longer comfortable being around you. I can't marry you. I'm breaking off the engagement."

"You *bitch!*"

Alison says, "Real classy, Nicki. Thanks for putting the cap on our special day."

"I don't appreciate your sarcasm, Alison. Your son *raped* me last night."

"*Shut up!*" Michael shouts, "or I'll fucking *kill* you!"

"How sweet of you to say, Michael. But your days of intimidating me are over. I'm sorry for the timing of that announcement, and for what else I've got to say."

Jess suddenly comes to life: "*I'll* tell them: Nicki and I are driving to Louisville this afternoon to move her things from Michael's apartment."

"Bullshit!" Michael says. "You're not taking anything without my approval."

"Really Michael?" Jess says. "Like I'd let her take your shit? Like she'd want it in the first place? You should be thankful she's willing

61

to tell the insurance guy about the rope around Daddy's neck instead of filing rape charges."

"I never raped you," he says to me. "Not even close."

Jess says, "Mom, are you okay with me and Nicki going to Louisville? We'll spend the night, come back tomorrow, and she can meet Mr. Blass and tell him about the rope."

As if I'm not even here, Alison says: "I'm sure Nicki can move her things out of Michael's apartment without your help. Also, I see no reason for her returning to Lexington. I'm sure our family has had quite enough of Nicki Hill for one lifetime."

As I study Alison's cold, angry face it's hard to imagine she was ever warm and loving to her husband. But she had to be, back in the day, or she never would have gotten that magnificent diamond on her finger. I try to picture her caught in the throes of passion screaming: *Oh God! Oh...Oh YES! Oh! Fuck me! Fuck me! FUCK me! Oh...I'm...I'm cumming! Oh God! Oh, Oh my GOD!*

"I don't have a ride," I say.

"Neither does Jessie," Alison says, "which is another good reason she should stay here."

I shrug. "I guess I can call a cab. What about Mr. Blass? I'm still happy to tell what I know. Maybe it'll help you with your case."

"I suppose if Mr. Blass wants to talk to you badly enough he'll either pick up the phone or drive to Louisville."

"Okay. By the way, you're welcome."

"If your story's true, I shouldn't *have* to thank you."

Michael says, "Lock my apartment when you leave, and don't bother returning the key. I'll change the locks when I get home."

"Fine."

Jess says, "I'll help you pack your stuff."

"Thanks."

As we enter the elevator, she laughs. "Omigod, Nicki! You were amazing!"

"You stole my *panties?*"

She grins. "Yup. But didn't you love the way I wove it into that story about Daddy?"

"Very impressive. But those are my favorite pair. I spent weeks looking for them."

"Next time we meet I'll wear them and we can swap."

"You mean with whatever I'm wearing that day?"

"Yup."

"In other words, I'll always be short a pair."

She laughs. "Exactly."

We exit the elevator, walk to the room, and I hold the key card in front of the door knob till it clicks. Once inside I say, "You stopped me from telling them about us. Why?"

"If I admitted I loved you they'd think *I* stole your panties, not Daddy."

"You're not upset what this blatant lie will do to his reputation?"

She laughs again. "I'm sorry. Are we still talking about the forty-two-year-old man who hanged himself and was found naked, covered in jizz, with his hand on his erect penis while watching babysitter porn? You think it matters if the insurance company thinks he stole your *panties?*"

"Good point. Wait. *Babysitter* porn? What's that?"

"Trust me, you don't want to know. But the panty story bolsters the accidental death claim, and let me tell you, it's a lot of money."

I smile at her use of the word bolster, and recall her saying pronouncement earlier this morning. She's truly quite intelligent, and I remind myself to never talk down to her. But she's brought up an interesting point I've been wondering about, so I ask: "How much is the death benefit, exactly?"

"Four million."

"Instead of two?"

"No. Four million *extra* for accidental death. Eight million in all."

"Wow."

"Yup, I'm rich. Aren't you glad we're a couple?"

"Absolutely! But I'd be just as glad if you were dirt poor."

"Right answer!"

"You think your mom will let us keep seeing each other?"

"How's she gonna stop us?"

"Lots of ways. And since we're breaking several laws, we'll need a private way to talk."

"Like Snapchat?"

"Like throwaway phones."

"You mean like drug dealers use?"

I nod.

"Where can I get one?"

"Anywhere: drug stores, gas stations, discount stores."

"Can't the cops trace them by matching the purchase to surveillance videos?"

"Possibly, which is why you'll pay a total stranger to buy it for you while you wait from a distance."

"Sounds like you've done this before."

I dig into my suitcase and show her my throwaway phone.

She grins. "This is gonna be *awesome*!"

I tuck the phone back in my suitcase, then pull her to me and we share a few moments of intimacy that leaves us wanting more. Then we gather my things, pack my suitcase, and head to the elevators. When we get to the lobby four people are waiting for us: Alison, Michael, and Police Detectives Broadus and Rudd.

"If there's nothing pressing," Broadus says, "we'd like to ask you a few questions."

"About David?" I say.

"Bingo."

"I've told you everything I know."

He rolls his eyes. "That may be the biggest lie I've heard in my entire career. A career filled with liars."

"Is that how you got so good at it?"

Detective Rudd stifles a laugh.

Broadus says, "How about we go somewhere and have a private chat?"

I look at Michael and Alison but *feel* Jessie staring at me from the side. "Anything you've got to say can be said in front of the Thornes. It'll save me the trouble of repeating it to them after you leave."

The detectives exchange a look, then Broadus says, "You're gonna want these questions to remain confidential as long as possible."

I smile. "Ask whatever you want. I've got nothing to hide."

Broadus shrugs. "Fair enough. Let's start with the comment you made to me yesterday afternoon."

"Okay."

"You said you only met David Thorne once, approximately three months ago, in a coffee shop."

"That's right."

"Then how did your nude photos wind up on his cell phone?"

Chapter 15

"THAT'S IMPOSSIBLE!" I say, but my words are punctuated by a vicious slap to the side of my face delivered by Jessie Thorne that causes me to spin forward so abruptly I lose my balance and stumble into Detective Rudd's arms. As he helps me regain my posture, I say, "Thanks for the vote of trust, Jess."

"Thanks for fucking my father and lying about it," she responds, icily.

I can't even imagine what Michael must be thinking, and have zero desire to see his face. But I *am* studying Alison's, and note she doesn't appear to be overly surprised.

God, I hate getting slapped! I've been punched, struck with objects, had my face pushed against walls, and lots worse. But nothing stings more than a hard slap. The moment of impact is like multiple bee stings, and within seconds the nerve endings in the entire area are screaming for relief, giving the whole side of your face the feeling it's swelling like a balloon. Add to that the ringing it causes in your ears, the headache, the involuntary tearing from the eyes, and you've got all the ingredients for a lousy half-hour.

But the tears are the worst.

Even though they're a natural response, they make you look like a wimp. Like you can't handle a slap from a 15-year-old girl. I want these bastards off my face, but wiping them would mean I'd have to acknowledge them. And I'm supposed to be tough.

Broadus says, "Would you like to see them?"

"What?"

"The naked photos."

I take a deep breath. "Yes, please."

He hands me the phone and I swipe the screen as I view them one after the other.

Michael says, "Jesus, Nicki, how many *are* there?"

I hand the phone back to Broadus, saying, "I don't know, Michael, I didn't count them just now. But *you* should know the exact number. You're the one who took them."

Broadus, looking genuinely surprised, says, "May I show them to Michael?"

"Why not? He's seen them many times, I'm sure."

I don't know if Michael realizes we're all staring at his face as he flips through the photos, but what's interesting—and a compliment to me—he doesn't stop till he's viewed the last one. He hands the phone back to Broadus, who says, "*You* took these photos?"

Michael nods.

Jess says, "Then how did they get on Daddy's phone?"

"Good question," I say. "Got an answer for us Michael?"

"I guess he must have gone through my phone and saw them and forwarded them to his."

Jessie hugs me. "I'm so sorry, Nicki."

"It's okay. Just one more example of your brother destroying my life."

"Fuck you!" Michael says.

"Yeah. Fuck me. And you sure did, didn't you? You begged me a thousand times to let you take those pictures, and when I finally agreed you promised no one would ever see them because of your privacy setting. And now we learn your father's been staring at them for God knows how long, not to mention these detectives and half the police department."

Rudd says, "Miss Hill, I can assure you—"

"Oh, shut up, Detective. I know how these things work. Within days these pictures will be all over the Internet because of your leering incompetence. Yesterday David Thorne accidentally hanged himself, or committed suicide. Either way I doubt it's part of your job description to find out why, but that's exactly what you've chosen to do. And for some reason you came to the instant conclusion he and I must have been having an affair. Well, we weren't. And even if we *had* been, what difference does it make to the police? The man clearly wasn't *murdered*. Meanwhile, you've taken every opportunity to undermine my relationship with the family to the point I'm no longer welcome in their home."

"Poor Nicki," Michael says, holding up his thumb and index finger like it's the world's tiniest violin. "You know what this is, Nicki?"

"You, masturbating?"

Everyone laughs, including Alison.

"Fuck you, bitch!" he snarls.

"Never again, Michael."

Jessie says, "Can I wait with you till your taxi shows up?"

"Thanks. I'd like that." I look at Broadus. "Anything else, Detective?"

He says, "Actually, there is. In fact, we're just getting started." He looks around, notices the furniture grouping by the large window where we sat a half hour ago. "How about we sit over there?"

"Not enough chairs."

"Detective Rudd and I will stand."

As we take our seats Broadus says, "You quit your job last month."

Michael says, "Not true. She called her boss yesterday before we left town."

"She may have *told* you that," Broadus says, "But she *did* quit her job. Correct, Miss Hill?"

I shrug. "Not last month. Two weeks ago. Is that a crime?"

Michael says, "You called them yesterday before we left. I *heard* you."

"I faked it."

"You quit your *job*?"

"I did."

"Why?"

I look at Detective Broadus. I know where this is going, I just don't want to say it. So he says it for me: "Nicki recently came into a large sum of money."

If you could see the looks on the Thorne family's faces you'd laugh. But I'm not laughing.

"How much money are we talking about?" Michael asks.

Broadus says, "One-point-two million dollars."

Chapter 16

ALISON SAYS, "WHETHER Nicki came into money or not is her business. She and Michael are no longer engaged, so I'm not sure why you're involving us in—"

Her face suddenly contorts and turns an angry shade of crimson. "You fucking bitch!"

Jess says, "*Jesus*, Mom! What's your *problem?*"

"You want to know my problem? I just realized why we're part of this discussion. It's because David—your *father*—gave Nicki the money. Am I right, Detective?"

"Indeed you are, Mrs. Thorne. That's very perceptive."

Michael jumps to his feet, tries to attack me, but Jess gets between us in the nick of time. Detective Rudd works him back in his chair and places a hand on Michael's shoulder to keep him from trying it again.

"Care to explain, Miss Hill?" Broadus says.

"If you're asking why David Thorne cashed out his Index Fund investment and had it transferred to my personal account, I can only tell you what he told me. But why should I?"

"Because it looks like blackmail."

"To whom?"

"The police."

"Are you saying David killed himself because I was blackmailing him?"

"Not yet. Not *officially*. But you have to admit it seems plausible."

"If I blackmailed him, and he paid the money, why would he kill himself?"

"Maybe you wanted more."

"If that were the case, wouldn't he have left a note to explain his actions?"

"You tell me."

"Fine. Yes. He would have left a note. And he *wouldn't* have been naked, with his hand on his dick, watching porn at the time of the hanging."

Alison winces at my mention of the position of David's hand. I'd like to say that remark just slipped out in the heat of the moment, but my choice of words was quite calculated. I won't be called a fucking bitch by Alison on the basis of pure conjecture, so I purposely hit her where it hurts. What David was doing at the time of his hanging is a very sensitive subject to her. Apart from the embarrassment, it tells the world their sex life wasn't what it should have been. Autoerotic asphyxiation is awfully extreme behavior for a wealthy guy from the estates of Lexington who has a dream life, dream wife, and perfect family.

What I'm about to say won't make a bit of difference to the detectives, since they've already made up their minds. But having been accused of something I didn't do, I should at least put forth a defense, so I say: "I didn't quit my job because of the money. I quit because my boss kept trying to put his hands on me. I didn't tell Michael because I was afraid he'd go there and make a scene."

Naturally, Broadus completely ignores my response. Instead, he points to the bank of elevators and says: "A few minutes ago you stood right there and told us you've got nothing to hide. Still feel that way?"

"Of course. It's the reason I keep answering your questions truthfully instead of hiring a lawyer."

"Then tell us why Mr. Thorne deposited $1.2 million into your checking account."

"He was paying me to break up with Michael."

"*What?*" Michael says.

"He wanted me for himself."

Michael recoils in horror, starts coughing uncontrollably. Meanwhile, Alison's eyes have narrowed to angry slits. Only Jess remains calm, waiting for my explanation, and so I offer it: "I never slept with David and never agreed to. But when I met him at the coffee shop that day, instead of trying to talk me into going back to Michael he told me he's loved me from the day we met and wanted to be with me. He said as long as Michael and I were together he didn't allow himself to tell me. But after I broke off the engagement, he felt there might be a chance. I had no idea he felt that way, and never understood how it could have happened till today."

"What happened today?"

"He had naked photos of me."

"And your panties," Jess says.

"Her panties?" Broadus says.

"Daddy stole a pair of Nicki's panties last March. He was obsessed with her."

I continue: "The day we met, David kept trying to talk me into dating him and said he was going to send me a huge sum of money to prove how serious he was. He said if I promised to give him a month I could keep the money even if things didn't work out between us. I told him I couldn't date him under any circumstances because not only was he Michael's dad, but also Alison's husband, and she and I were extremely close. At least we *were*. But David had the money wired to my account anyway, and when I got the notification from the bank, I told him it didn't matter. I refused to date him, and that's the truth."

"Worked out nicely for you," Alison says. "You made a cool $1.2 million for doing nothing."

"I didn't keep the money."

"What?"

Broadus says, "What did you do with it?"

"Surely you've checked."

"We haven't gotten that far yet."

"Well, when you do, you'll find I gave it to Michael."

Michael looks up. "What are you *talking* about?"

"When I turned your dad down, it destroyed him. I said I was flattered by his gesture, but I couldn't keep the money. I told him I was going back to you, and he was...I won't say *pleased*, but...pacified. He said he wanted me to keep the money and use it for our future. So I thought about it, but that didn't seem right because, what if we broke up again? So I asked your dad where the money came from and he told me about the index fund, and so I set up an account with that same company and put your name on it."

"You put $1.2 million into an account for *me?*"

"Actually, I put one million in your account, and put the rest in our joint checking account so you'd have enough money to pay the gift taxes."

The stars in Jessie' eyes say it all: she's found her soulmate.

Michael's less impressed. He asks Broadus, "How can I keep her from taking the two hundred thousand?"

"What do you mean?"

"She just broke up with me, and the money's in our joint account. She's obviously going to take it."

"Wow," I say. "Seriously Michael? Every time you open your mouth it proves I made the right decision to leave you." I reach into my handbag, hand him my checkbook for our joint account. "Here, Michael. The money's yours. I've always considered it yours."

Jess looks at her brother like he's turd on toast: "She's right Michael. You really blew it this time. Congratulations! You're officially the world's biggest asshole."

Broadus says, "Miss Hill? If you want to change any part of your story, now's the time."

"Why's that?"

"Because we're going to check everything you said."

"Please do."

Alison says "Nicki, I owe you an apology. If all this checks out as I'm sure it will, you'll have earned my respect, even as David has proven himself to be a total bastard."

"Thanks Alison. I've always loved your family, even David. I'm just sorry for everything that happened."

"It's not your fault," Jess says, and everything's cool till Broadus asks, "Who called whom?"

"Excuse me?"

"A few minutes ago you said David wired the money. You told him you were going back to Michael, and David said to keep the money and use it for your future together."

"So?"

"How did that conversation take place? Did you call him or meet him?"

"I—he called me."

"Really? Because we checked his phone records, and your number doesn't show up anywhere."

"Maybe he erased it."

"Maybe. But you know what he *didn't* erase?" He looks around. "Anyone?"

Michael says, "The naked photos."

Broadus shakes his head. "He didn't erase the dozens of calls he made and received from a number we can't identify. It appears to be a throwaway."

Without looking in my direction, Jess asks, "What's a throwaway?"

"A pre-paid phone."

"You mean like drug dealers use?"

"That's right."

"You think Daddy was a *drug* dealer?"

"No, but he was conversing regularly with someone who didn't want his—or her—identity known. Have any of you been using a pre-paid phone?"

No one speaks up, which is pretty interesting, since Jessie knows I have a throwaway phone in my suitcase and I happen to know Alison has been using one for months.

"How about *you*, Miss Hill?"

I shake my head.

Broadus says, "Reason I ask, the day the money was transferred to your account, David made two calls to that number in the space of thirty minutes: just before, and just after the transfer was completed."

"So?"

"Considering there's no record of you and him calling each other, I'd say that's quite a coincidence, wouldn't you?" He removes his phone from his pocket, selects a number from his call list, and says: "I'm going to call that number right now. Wouldn't it be funny if we hear it ringing somewhere nearby?"

"Hilarious."

Once again I feel Jessie's eyes on me, or at least on my suitcase, as Broadus presses the key. And though we're all listening intently, I already know the phone he's calling can't possibly be heard ringing, since I stomped it into pieces and flushed it down the toilet in the women's bathroom at the Chevron station at Exit 53 on I-64 outside Frankfort, Kentucky, while Michael was gassing the car up yesterday. The throwaway phone in my suitcase was purchased last week by a teenager I met in a shopping center next to a Wal-Mart, and hasn't been used yet. When Broadus ends his call, I ask, "Was there anything else, Detective?"

"Yes. Do you off-hand know your social security number?"

"No."

"You don't?"

"I do, but I'm tired of playing your stupid games. If you want it badly enough, look it up in your law-enforcement database."

"Actually, I did that last night. And you know what I learned?"

Of course I do. But I wait for him to say it:

"Nicki Hill doesn't exist."

Poor Michael. Despite realizing he's just become a millionaire, he's having a rough time, evidenced by the look of total bewilderment on his face. He points his finger in my direction and feebly says, "She's right there."

Broadus says, "She might *call* herself Nicki Hill, but her real name's Katie Walker."

My eyes go straight to Alison's face to see how she reacts, and all I can say is, either the lady doesn't know the name (which I doubt) or she deserves an Oscar. Apart from the split second her eyes may have widened, it's hard to tell. But what strikes me as curious, for all the astonishing police work Detective Broadus has accomplished in the last twenty-plus hours—and let's give the man his due, he's done an amazing job—even *he* has no idea who Katie Walker is, and why this revelation has just become a total game-changer.

Part Two:

Michael, Jessie, and Alison

Chapter 1

Michael

EIGHTEEN MONTHS AGO I was sitting in a Starbucks waiting for a 22-year-old divorced aerobics instructor named Chrissy to show up and rock my world. We met on a dating site, but she obviously changed her mind about me because she never showed. At the point she was officially 30-minutes late, a stunning brunette (think: Alicia Vikander, the actress) jumped into the seat across from me and whispered, "Act like you know me."

"Excuse me?"

"There's a guy," she said, as if that explained everything.

I started to look over my shoulder to see who this guy was, but she said, "Don't do that. You'll tip him off."

"To what?"

"The fact I'm ditching him."

"Is he your boyfriend?"

"*Excuse* me? You honestly think I'd go out with a guy like that on *purpose?*"

"I have no idea. I haven't actually seen him yet."

"Well *I* just saw him, and I've got a bad feeling."

"Fair enough. Can I ask you something?"

"Please do! It'll make us look like a couple."

"If you keep sitting here, am I apt to get beat up?"

"Do you think I'd put you in that sort of position?"

"I truly don't know."

"Want me to leave?"

"No."

She smiled. "I'm not telling you my name."

"That's okay. I'm Michael Thorne."

"Hi Michael. Thanks for letting me sit here. Don't worry, I'll bail as soon as it's safe."

"No need to rush." I paused. "Why are you afraid to tell me your name?"

"I'm not. I just know you'll forget it."

"That's impossible. You're literally the prettiest girl I've ever spoken to."

"Thanks."

"Tell me your name. I'm dying to know."

She stared at me a moment, then said, "Nicki Hill. Say it three times."

After I did she said, "You've been great. Want my digits?"

"Absolutely!" She took my phone, typed her name and number into my contact list, then stood, walked to the front door, opened it, looked in all directions, and left.

By then I was completely under her spell.

From that day to this we've argued 90% of our waking hours, broken up more times than I can count, got engaged twice, and in all these months I've fucked her exactly—don't laugh—three times. We've done a lot of fooling around, meaning I get to touch her from the waist up on a semi-regular basis, but not below the waist, because she's got serious issues.

How serious?

Let's put it this way: every time I tried to touch her private area she broke up with me. As for the three times we had actual intercourse? None lasted more than a minute, and in all cases she locked herself in the bathroom afterward. The first two times she vomited, and last night she accused me of rape. On the bright side, she loves my sister Jess, and my mom, and they adore her. And when she and I are alone and she's in a good mood (which is rare) she's funny as hell, fun to be around, gives great hand jobs, and has no problem peeing in front of me or walking around the house completely naked. I mentioned the peeing not because I'm weird, but because you'd assume any girl who doesn't want to be touched below the waist would also feel uncomfortable peeing in front of me. But strangely, it's not an issue.

Chapter 2

FOR THE LONGEST time I had no idea why Nicki was so freaked out about the touching. Then Mom told me about Nicki's childhood, and how she bounced from one foster family to the next, after being subjected to the worst abuse imaginable. It broke my heart. I decided whatever Nicki's shortcomings might be, the good outweighed the bad. And until yesterday we'd been getting along better than ever. She was even considering seeing a therapist to help her with her intimacy issues.

What's that they say? What a difference a day makes? Yesterday we were in the same coffee shop where we met, laughing and having a great time...then Mom called to say Dad hanged himself, and from there everything turned to shit and Nicki morphed back into Crazy Nicki. It started the minute we got to Mom and Dad's house, when the detectives separated us and asked us tons of questions about Nicki's relationship with my dad.

My *dad*?

Next thing you know, Mom's convinced Nicki's been having an affair with Dad. I knew better, but didn't want to tell her about Nicki's intimacy issues. Then last night we were in bed and I was upset and Nicki was being super nice, trying to comfort me. With all the emotions swirling through my brain, I went for it. The entire event lasted maybe forty seconds, and as always I didn't get to finish because she rushed to the bathroom and locked herself inside until I fell asleep. A couple hours later I noticed she'd left the room and I went looking for her and found her in the hotel lobby, telling Jess I raped her.

And Jess totally bought it.

That was the final straw. I get that Nicki has serious intimacy issues, but I dare her to show one bruise or mark anywhere on her body that would offer the slightest suggestion of rape.

But that's Nicki.

I'll stop short of calling her a liar, because who knows what goes on in her mind during the act of sex? But as God is my witness, I didn't rape her, and nor was I rough with her. Was I excited? Yes. After all, she didn't retch. Did I approach the event with great enthusiasm? Certainly. After all, she didn't throw a fit when I touched her down there.

Mom said it best a while ago: since yesterday afternoon we've been on an emotional roller coaster. Between Dad hanging himself while jacking off, and the revelations from Jess about how he stole Nicki's panties last March, and all the crap Detective Broadus has accused Nicki of, and her bombshell that Dad paid her more than a million dollars to dump me and run off with him—it's just too much to deal with. But through it all, Nicki's good qualities were on display. Astonishingly—if she's to be believed—instead of keeping all the money Dad gave her, she transferred it to me. And the crazy thing is, I believe her. I absolutely do. Because one thing I'll say about Nicki: she's immune to money. Never once has she asked me for any, or asked about our family's money, or what my dad did for a living, or even what sort of assets or trust funds I might have.

She doesn't have a greedy bone in her body.

Chapter 3

I'LL TELL YOU something else about Nicki: my dad was a very nice-looking guy who looked years younger than his true age of forty-two. And while that's a big age difference for Nicki, I doubt many women would turn down $1.2 million to have an affair with my dad. True, she wouldn't have wanted the sex. But Dad probably would have settled for what she'd offer, same as I have, and I say that because he gave her the money anyway. And of course, Nicki could have taken it and left me, had she wanted to.

But she gave it to me.

So here we are, in the hotel lobby, and Nicki's packed her suitcase and—big surprise—she's leaving me again, and I'm coming across very badly because I was already in a foul mood *before* she accused me of raping her. Detective Broadus keeps hammering her with accusations, and even though she's acing her responses, I'm learning one shocking fact after another. But to Nicki's credit, even though I've been ugly to her, and Mom cursed her, and Jess *slapped* her, here's Nicki, telling Broadus how much she loves our family.

So I'm going to do what I always do: give her some space and time and take her back the moment she's ready. And when she moves back in I'll try like hell not to touch her below the waist.

Which reminds me...

Chapter 4

ONE OF THE most peculiar things about Nicki is the way she references things she wants to avoid. For example, she's repulsed by testicles. Doesn't want to think about them, hear about them, and especially doesn't want to see or touch them, even by accident. In Nicki's perfect world, there'd *be* no testicles! And yet she calls them "friends," as in: "I can't stand your friends." So instead of saying, "I'll give you a hand job if you cover your balls," she'll say, "I might give you some relief tonight, but I don't want to see your friends."

Even weirder, instead of saying "I can't stand intercourse," she'll say, "I don't want children," which is very confusing when we're out with friends and they ask, "Why are you guys always breaking up?" And she'll say, "Michael wants children, and I don't. Every fight we've ever had boils down to him wanting children." And then they look at me, like, "Jesus, Michael. You've got this incredibly beautiful girl and she wants it to be just the two of you, and you're fighting about *kids?* Are you *crazy?*"

–I just shrug and say nothing, content to love her, and keep her secrets.

But that said, I'm stunned about Dad. You think you know someone after spending a lifetime with him, and suddenly learn he's into kinky sex, lusts after your fiancée, steals her panties, ogles her nude photos, and pays her a fortune to leave you and run off with him. I swear, if I'd found out all this shit before yesterday Dad wouldn't have had time to kill himself. I would have strangled him with my bare hands.

Detective Broadus has hit Nicki with everything but the kitchen sink, and she's killing it for one simple reason: she's innocent. But he's made it his life's mission to make her look guilty of something. Did she have an affair with Dad? No. Then why are her nude pictures on his phone? I took the pictures, Dad transferred them to his phone. Why did she quit her job? Her boss came onto her. I believe her, it's happened before. Why didn't she tell me? I let it slide the first time, but like she said, she knew I'd go to her former workplace and make a scene.

Now it gets interesting:

Chapter 5

DAD GAVE HER $1.2 *million*? Yes. Was she blackmailing him? No. Can she prove it? Yes: it's not blackmail if she didn't ask for the money, and didn't keep it. And here's the kicker: she gave it to *me*, which was the biggest mistake she could have possibly made. Why? Because Dad gave the money to Nicki, not me, so Nicki owes the gift taxes. Yes, she transferred the money to me, but that doesn't eliminate *her* tax burden. She still owes the IRS the gift taxes on $1.2 million! So do I, since she transferred the money to me. But luckily I now have $200,000 with which to pay my tax burden.

In other words, I have complete and total power over her future: if she leaves me, she won't be able to afford to pay her taxes and the IRS will put her in jail. But if she marries me, we'll pay the taxes as a married couple.

She's in a tight spot, and has but one way out: marrying me.

Poor Nicki has no clue what she's done, or how it could affect her. But fortunately for her, I still love her and want to marry her.

Now Broadus is asking for Nicki's social security number, and claims she's not who she says she is, but rather someone named Katie Walker. So I immediately start wracking my brain, trying to figure out if this is one of Nicki's weird things, like how she claims not to want children, except that she's telling Detective Broadus she can call herself whatever she wants as long as she's not using a fake name to break any laws. That doesn't sound right to me, but surprisingly, he agrees with her and admits there are no outstanding warrants anywhere in the country for either name. Still, he asks why she feels the need to use a fake name.

Nicki responds, "I'm no longer that girl. I wanted to put that name and that life behind me."

Broadus says, "Then why not make it legal? Why not go to court and have your name legally changed?"

And Nicki says, "I planned to. I just haven't gotten around to it yet."

I ask, "How long have you been using the alias?"

Detective Broadus answers for her: "Eighteen months."

Which of course is the exact amount of time I've known her.

Mom says, "Detective, I appreciate all the hard work you've put into this, but Nicki's clearly got nothing to do with my husband's death. She's a friend of the family, and I regret that your comments last night made us doubt her."

Broadus says, "Miss Walker?"

Nicki says, "If you want my cooperation you'll call me Nicki Hill."

"Very well. Miss Hill, would you be willing to take a polygraph?"

"About what?"

"I'd like to see what the polygraph says about you having a sexual relationship with David Thorne, or if you were blackmailing him."

We all look at Nicki, who says, "If I take the test and pass it will you accept the result and guarantee no police officer or detective will ever question me about this again?"

"Absolutely."

"Will you put it in writing?"

"We don't work that way."

"Then no. Sorry."

"Why not?"

"Because it's one more thing, and I haven't done anything wrong. You know for a fact I wasn't even in Lexington when David hanged himself, and nor did I have an affair with him, and nor did I ask him for money, and nor did I keep the money he sent. I've never committed a crime and never used my old or new names for illegal purposes."

"You didn't want the money David offered?"

"Of course I did. But I'm not a prostitute."

"I didn't claim you were."

"You claimed I was blackmailing him."

"Weren't you?"

"Of course not."

"You said you never asked him to pay you the money."

"That's correct."

"Yet he wired the money to your personal account."

"So?"

"If you weren't blackmailing him, how did he know your account information?"

"What do you mean?"

"How did he know your personal bank account number and the bank's routing number? It seems to me the only way he'd know that is if you told him where to wire the money."

Chapter 6

NICKI ROLLS HER eyes because once again Detective Broadus is making her look bad when she's done nothing wrong.

"I'll take this one," I say. "Dad does all our taxes. Last year he offered to do Nicki's, and she didn't want to impose, but this year she said yes. So he had all her financial information, including her checking account number."

Broadus frowns and looks at Rudd.

Rudd shakes his head.

I can see it in their eyes: they're done. Mom sees it too, and says, "Detective? Please. Let it go. We just want to move on."

Broadus says, "It doesn't bother you that your husband sent this young, good-looking lady a million dollars?"

"Of course it does," she snapped. "But it bothers me a lot more that my husband was a pervert who stole her panties and drooled over her naked pictures and wanted to run off with her, and it bothers me he got naked and hanged himself and that my daughter had to find him like that, and..." her voice trails off, and Detective Broadus says, "I'm sorry, ma'am. To be honest, the reason I've pursued this line of questioning so aggressively is the department only gave us 24 hours to wrap this case up, and because of the...circumstances surrounding your husband's death we knew the insurance company would be all over us to be as thorough as possible."

Detective Rudd adds, "Although we have some lingering doubts about Miss Hill's influence on your husband's actions, we can't pursue her personal and financial records without extending our time frame, and the scope of our investigation. If you're satisfied we've done our job, our report will show it's our opinion Mr. Thorne's death was accidental."

"Thank you," Mom says. "And yes, we're satisfied you've covered all the bases."

Jess says, "Detective Broadus? I think you owe Nicki an apology."

Broadus says, "That would be pushing it."

Nicki says, "Thanks, Jess. Detective Broadus? No hard feelings. In fact, if anything ever happens to me I hope you and Detective Rudd get the case. But with regard to *this* case, I've done nothing wrong."

"Let's put it this way, Miss Hill: if you did, you got away with it."

I can't help but notice the effect his words have on Mom: she's visibly agitated. And when the detectives finally leave, she says, "Nicki, you and I need to talk. Just the two of us. Would that suit you?"

And Nicki says, "I'm looking forward to it."

And Mom says, "Let's go to my room."

Chapter 7

Jessie

THE FIRST TIME Michael brought Nicki home to meet the family we were worried as hell because all his previous girlfriends turned out to be worse than zombie crypt creepers. But Nicki made such a good impression we couldn't believe his good fortune.

"What's your opinion?" Daddy asked, after her first family interrogation.

"I love her," I said, and if I didn't mean it literally at the time, I soon did. Nicki built an instant rapport with me by doing something no brother's girlfriend—or anyone else—would ever do: after dinner she said, "Jessie, I'd like to get to know you better. Would you show me your room?"

Michael said something stupid, like, "Her room's a disaster," but Nicki instinctively knew that was the perfect way to discover the real me. So she followed me into my room, closed the door behind us, sat on my bed and said, "I'm gonna tell you something about me that no one in the whole world knows. Can I trust you to keep my secret?"

"Of course!" I said, with eyes as big as plates.

She patted the bed for me to sit beside her, and said, "Remember at dinner when we told you guys how we met?"

"Yes," and to prove I'd been paying attention I added, "Michael set up an online date with an aerobics instructor who stood him up and you also had a date scheduled at the same coffee shop a half hour later with a goon you'd never met and you took one look at him and wanted to hide, but there was nowhere to go, so you sat with Michael until the goon guy finally left."

Nicki smiled. "Exactly." Then she said, "Don't tell anyone, but that entire story is bullshit."

"What do you mean?"

"I catfished Michael."

"Whaaa?"

"There *was* no Chrissy the aerobics instructor. I made her up."

"Wait! You're saying—"

"The profile, the pictures, the online conversations with Michael...all phony."

"Omigod!"

Nicki laughed. "And of course, I didn't have a date with the goon. In fact, there *was* no goon. I just pretended there was."

"Does Michael know?"

"Nope. Like I said, I've never told anyone. If you decide to tell him or your parents, you'll scorch me."

I thought about it a long time, then said, "Why did you tell me that?"

"Because I really like you, Jess, and want us to be friends. I'm taking a chance on you. Maybe I'm wrong, but I feel I can trust you."

"You can, I promise."

"I believe you. So every time I come here, we'll get together, and I'll tell you a secret."

"Does that mean I have to tell you *my* secrets?"

"No. But it *does* mean you can tell me anything, and know in your heart that no matter what happens, I'll never tell anyone."

"Wow."

How could I not find her beyond amazing after an introduction like *that*? In less than an hour I felt closer to Nicki than I did to most of my life-long friends. And so I told her some of the silly things that didn't really matter, little confessions about the stuff me and my friends had done, and she asked about my closest friends, and I told her about Ellie and Holly, and about how smooth Holly is with the boys and how awkward I am, and in the visits that followed, as we got closer and closer I confided bigger things, like how I smoked weed a couple of times and got sick, and how some of my friends did a line of coke at a party and made fun of me for backing out. And how me, Ellie, and Holly snuck out one night so Ellie could hook up with some random guy she met online who turned out to be a 30-year-old pervert, and how we realized he could have killed or raped us, and how terrified we were at the time, but laugh about it now.

Last March Nicki and Michael came for the weekend, and as always she and I talked in my room for hours, and she asked me about my friends, and I told her how cute Holly is and how brave Ellie is, and about all the friendship promises we made to each other. I told her how the guys at school have been coming on to us, and how Holly, me, and Ellie had a sleepover and snuck some beers and worked on our kissing techniques by kissing each other and pretending we were kissing boys, and how we couldn't stop laughing about it, and how we took pictures and called each other gay and threatened to out each other on Snapchat, and—

"Except that you weren't pretending with Holly," she said.

"What do you mean?"

"You enjoyed kissing her."

For a split second I was mad. But the way Nicki kept looking at me with those big green eyes I could tell she really cared. Still, I didn't want her to think less of me, so I was about to tell her she was wrong about my feelings, but then she said, "I wish Holly didn't like the boys so much."

"Why?"

"Because she'd be perfect for you."

"I'm not gay," I said, indignantly.

"I never said you *were*, Jess. But love is love."

"What's *that* supposed to mean?"

"It means love is so fucking hard to find, I think our hearts should be open to all possibilities. Ask me if I'd consider having sex with a girl."

"*Would* you?"

"Absolutely!"

"Whaaa? *You?*"

"Absolutely. Assuming I had feelings for her. And as my friend, I'd hope you'd be okay with that."

"Of course I would. But...what about Michael?"

"What about him?"

"Would you ever cheat on him?"

"If I answer honestly, will it be our secret?"

"Of course! Always!"

Chapter 8

NICKI SAID, "MICHAEL and I fight all the time. It's exhausting. If I had to place odds on us lasting another month, I'd bet no."

"How come?"

"He wants to get married and have kids, and I don't. So yeah, if the right person came along, I'd probably cheat on him."

"What if that person was a girl?"

"A *girl?*"

"Or, you know, a woman."

"I hope it *is* a woman...or a girl...of legal age."

"Sixteen's legal in Kentucky!" I blurted out.

She arched her brows. "Is it?"

I felt my face turning red. "I think so."

"If the girl was *that* much younger than me I'd have to be convinced she found me super attractive."

"How could she not? You're gorgeous!"

"You're the one who's gorgeous, Jess. I'd *kill* to have your legs. Not to mention your cheekbones."

I blushed like an idiot, then shocked myself by asking: "Will you promise me something?"

"Probably. But I need to know what it is first."

"If you ever cheat on Michael, will you tell me?"

She frowned. "That could put me in a tough situation, since he's your brother."

"It wouldn't matter. I'd take your side no matter what."

"Then...yes," she said.

"But I want every last detail," I said. "No matter how small. You can't leave *anything* out."

"Of course. But in that case you'll have to make *me* a promise."

"Like what?"

"The first time *you* have sex..."

"*Omigod!*" I screamed, and we laughed so hard Michael knocked on the door and asked if everything was all right. And all I could think about from that day on was how Nicki—not Holly—was the one who was perfect for me. And that night when she and Michael went to a bar I snuck in their room and stole the cutest pair of panties from her suitcase, and never told her about it till today. And the way I spun it, making it look like Daddy stole them, was probably worth an extra four million dollars of insurance money for my family, so it turned out to be a good thing.

By the way, Nicki was right about her and Michael: the very next month they *did* break up. She came to the house to talk to Mom and me about it. After talking to Mom out on the gazebo, she came to my room and we visited and she could tell I was upset and asked me why and that's when I told her that Mom was cheating on Daddy.

Chapter 9

"ARE YOU *SURE?*" Nicki asked.

"Yup."

"Does your dad know?"

"I don't think so."

"How'd you find out?"

I told her how Mom has a secret phone I found by accident, and even though she had a privacy code on it, it was simple to figure out as she stupidly used her birth year. "She only used the phone for this guy and never erased the call history or any of their texts."

"Who's the guy?"

"One of our neighbors."

"Is he good looking?"

"God no! But if you ever read their texts you'd think he was George Clooney."

Nicki said, "Personally I don't find George Clooney attractive at all."

I laughed. "Me either. I was really just trying to think of someone old that Mom might think was good looking."

Last night I told Nicki two of my biggest secrets. I told her I loved her, and wanted to be with her, and I also told her I was adopted. I think the only secret I *haven't* told her or anyone else is the one I'll never tell, 'cause I don't want to hurt her feelings. It involves Daddy, and how two weeks ago he said never to trust Nicki.

"She's a master manipulator," he said. "Don't ever trust her." Of course I defended her, and he got furious and called Nicki the c-word and said, "She'll never step foot in this house again!" Of course, he'd been drinking heavily, and I know now that he had a huge crush on her, and this would have been around the time she turned him down after he sent her a ton of money to get her to leave Michael and run off with him, so it makes sense he'd be mad at her.

But that's all behind us now because Daddy hanged himself, and Michael sexually assaulted Nicki, and she decided to leave him once and for all, and I confessed my feelings for her, and she melted in my arms, and now we're hopelessly in love. And while I'm miserable about Daddy, I'm insanely happy about my new relationship with Nicki, whose actual name might be Katie, according to the jerk detective who's been harassing her since the moment he showed up to investigate Daddy's death. But I don't care if her name is Nicki, Katie, or Phineas and Ferb. I love her, and we're gonna be together forever.

At this exact moment Detective Broadus finally ended his witch hunt, and he and Detective Rudd just left. Mom asked Nicki if they could speak privately, and I can't wait to hear what that's all about. Of course, I won't have to wait long, since I know Nicki will tell me every last detail soon enough.

My biggest problem is Michael. Ever since last night he's been treating Nicki like shit. But when she gave him her checkbook he started acting differently. I know he's gonna do what he always does: beg her to come back.

But this time it's not gonna work. This time she's got me. And I'm not gonna let anything come between me and Nicki. Not Michael, not Mom, not anyone.

Chapter 10

Alison

I'M IN MY hotel room staring at Nicki Hill, the young woman I thought I knew. But it's not Nicki, it's Katie Walker, and she's staring back at me defiantly, daring me to say what we both know I'm thinking...and so I do: "How much does Michael know about your background?"

"Just the stuff you told him about the foster homes."

"How many times have you changed your name?"

"Are you including who I was before I became Katie Walker?"

"No."

"Then...just twice. I actually used the name Alison for a while."

"Alison what?"

"Henry."

"When was that?"

"The first time I got engaged."

"You were married?"

"No. It didn't work out."

"There's a shock."

"But the guy was hard to shake, so I became Nicki Hill. And then I met Michael."

"Nice catching up with you. You're quite the little slut, aren't you."

"Is that why you wanted to visit? So you could insult me?"

"Partly. But I really wanted to ask how you could *do* this to Michael. And why *would* you?"

"You know why."

I *do* know, Katie, I just can't believe it. "For more than a year you've—"

"Call me Katie again and I'll walk out that door. And while we're at it, let's be precise on the timeline: it's been eighteen months, three days, seventeen hours and..." she checks her phone. "Nine minutes since I started dating Michael. All torture."

"What is it you want?"

"Please don't insult me. You've pieced it together."

As I stare at Nicki's calm, beautiful face and try to imagine the severely damaged brain hiding behind her ever-innocent sea-green eyes, I think back to the moment I met her, knowing now, for the first time—who she is and what she's been up to from day one. It seems impossible she could have come across so shy, sweet, polite, and charming. That day she won my whole family over. And now she's shaking me down.

"How much?" I say.

"Two million."

It's all falling into place. "So you *were* blackmailing David."

"No. Everything I told Detective Broadus was 100% true. Um... with two exceptions. I know it hurts your ego to hear this, but your husband really did want to run off with me. He begged me to take the money."

"I don't believe you."

She shrugs.

"Nor do I believe he stole your panties."

She smiles. "I told *you* that story. Not Detective Broadus."

"So you admit you lied."

"It's to our mutual benefit that you get the extra four million, is it not?"

"How'd you get Jessie to back you up?"

"We're in love."

"What do you mean?"

"Think about it: all those hours alone in her bedroom with the door shut? How do *you* think my panties wound up under your daughter's mattress?"

My reaction is swift: I launch the hardest slap to her face I can muster, but she catches my hand in mid-air, crushes it in her grip, and slaps my face so hard with her other hand I barely maintain consciousness.

"Big mistake, Alison," she says. "I'm a lot tougher than I look. You'd understand that better if you'd suffered years of abuse like I have. Sorry about your hand."

She releases it and just in time, as I'm certain she was within seconds of breaking my fingers. She seems to have almost superhuman strength. I expect she could kill me with her bare hands.

With tears streaming down my cheeks I ask:

Chapter 11

"DID YOU EVER hit Michael that hard?"

"No. Unlike you, he never tried to hit me. Are you *crying*, Alison?"

"No. Were you crying when my 15-year-old slapped you?"

"No. But I hit harder."

"No shit you do!"

Nicki smiles.

I rub my rapidly-swelling face and ask, "If you told Broadus the truth about all but two things I assume one of the lies you told was about not having an affair with David."

"I didn't lie. I never touched your husband. I wouldn't *do* that."

"Well, you certainly touched my son. And apparently my *daughter*?"

"Yes and no. With regard to Michael, he and I never had what you'd call traditional sex. He tried, obviously, but I had no interest. Jessie's a different story. Our relationship is real, and physical, and I'm going to ask you to respect it."

"That will never happen," I say, fighting the urge to go for her throat.

"We don't have to be friends, Alison. But you do have to let Jess and I explore our relationship. Not that there's anything you can do about it. I mean, we're going to be together whether you like it or not."

"Nicki, you're a sick, fucking, degenerate..."

"I'm waiting for a noun, Alison. Surely there's a noun coming."

"...*Pedophile!*"

"Ouch."

"You knew she was underage. You could go to prison for what you've done."

"What have I done?"

"You just admitted molesting my underage daughter."

"*Did* I? Where's your proof?"

I grit my teeth. "You're cocky now, but she'll come to her senses. She'll rat you out soon enough. You're going to do hard time for this."

"We'll see."

If I had any sense, I'd remain calm. But when it comes to my daughter, I'll fight to the death. I may be too late to save her virginity, but I can certainly prevent this from happening again. All I have to do is...

"You're thinking about telling her who I am."

"Count on it," I sneer.

"It won't matter," she says. "Jess will take my side and you'll only make things worse for yourself. If you try to break us up she'll never forgive you."

"I'll take my chances."

"Of course you will. It's how you've lived your entire life."

"Fuck you, Nicki."

"Let's not be rude, Alison. You came here for answers, so I'll give you a few. Again, I'll reiterate I never touched David. I wouldn't do that, and you of all people should know that. And while I hate to keep repeating myself, I'll say it once again: I never blackmailed him. I wasn't trying to win David over, but he developed a massive crush on me, and you only have yourself to blame for that. If you'd been a better wife, he never would have looked my way. It makes me cringe to think he went through Michael's phone searching for photos. I'm sure he wasn't expecting to find nudity, but that's probably what gave him the courage to pursue me."

"David has proven himself to be a despicable pig," I say, "but you can't pin his behavior on me. You know nothing about our relationship. He didn't deserve it, but I was a wonderful wife. I was always there for him."

"*Were* you? Even while fucking his insurance agent?"

"*What?*"

"What do you think the insurance company would do if they knew you and Mr. Blass have been having a long-term affair? You think they might re-think your accidental death claim? I certainly do! And let's not forget you and Michael are already on the record lying about David's previous history of autoerotic activities."

"You can't prove that."

"Maybe not, but I can cast some serious doubt. I'm no expert, Alison, but I think your affair could cause you some problems. I wouldn't be surprised if *you're* the one doing prison time."

"Let's get back on point: two million makes this go away? Makes *you* go away? Forever?"

"Two million plus Jessie."

Chapter 12

"I WON'T SELL my daughter."

"I'm not asking you to. I'm only asking that you allow her to see me."

"That's child abuse. I'll go to prison first."

"I hope that's true, because if you're in prison, there'll be no one to keep us apart."

She's right. That would be a double loss. So I ask, "How much would I have to pay you to walk away from Jessie?"

"Wow. Now you sound like David."

I feel my face flush. "Hardly. According to you, David wanted you for himself."

"According to *me*? Look Alison, I'll admit you're extremely attractive for your age, and maybe you're right. Maybe David's interest in me had nothing to do with your shortcomings as a wife. But he absolutely offered me the money to have an affair, and I absolutely turned him down. And when I said I was going back to Michael, he told me to keep the money for our future. There was no affair and no blackmail."

"If you weren't denying it so strongly, I might believe you."

Nicki nods. "I can see why you'd say that. And I'm not sure why it's so important to me that you believe me. But if you don't, I suppose there's nothing more I can say to change your mind."

"Give me a number, Nicki. What will it take for you to break things off with Jessie, move away, and never contact us again?"

"Five million dollars."

Chapter 13

"FIVE *MILLION?* THAT'S impossible."

"I'm willing to entertain a counter offer."

"Two million five."

"Sorry."

As I look at her I remember something she said earlier that made me curious. "What were the exceptions?"

"Excuse me?"

"You said you were completely honest with Broadus, with two exceptions. What were they?"

"I told him I didn't have a throwaway phone. I do. It's in my suitcase. But unlike *your* throwaway phone, I've never used it."

"What's the other lie?"

"I kept the money."

"You didn't transfer it to Michael?"

"Of course not. That would make *me* liable for the gift taxes."

I smile. "Your first big mistake."

"You think?"

"Broadus will find out. He assured you he was going to check out your story."

"He was bluffing. Like he told us in the lobby they gave him twenty-four hours to wrap the case. I suppose if you tell him I kept the money he might try to prove I was blackmailing David, but my version's much stronger than his. And mine also happens to be true. Don't forget: Broadus saw my photos on David's phone. If I'd been fucking and blackmailing David, it'd be the other way around: *I'd* have photos of David and me on *my* phone."

"Look: you've already got $1.2 million. I'll pay you $2.8 million more. That's a cool $4 million. That's half the insurance proceeds."

"It's a pittance," she says. "You'll get $8 million from the insurance, tax free. The house and land are easily worth another $8 million, and I'm sure David's business is worth at least $20 million, possibly twice that. Not to mention your cars, checking accounts, savings accounts, jewelry, personal effects, and *his* IRA and investment accounts. I'll bet he owned more than one life insurance policy, too. I'd value his estate at forty to fifty million."

"You have no idea what he owns. He could be swimming in debt, for all you know."

"That's possible," she says, "but not likely. Because if David was swimming in debt he wouldn't have offered me $1.2 million to have an affair."

She's right of course. I stopped loving David years ago, but remained in the marriage for the sake of the kids and the lifestyle. Nicki's valuation of $50 million is surprisingly close, but doesn't include his inheritance. Then Nicki says, "And those numbers don't even reflect his inheritance. I'm guessing that's what, another hundred million?"

"How do you know about that?"

"Michael told me."

I frown. What a stupid thing to tell her...but of course he did. I'm sure he considered Nicki the catch of a lifetime and probably used that as bait early in the game.

"I'm not sure why Michael told you that, but he's way off base."

"You mean it's *more* than a hundred million?"

"Much less."

"Well, even if it's only $50 million, the five I'm asking is still a tiny portion."

"Let's be perfectly clear," I say. "If I offer you $3.8 million, plus the $1.2 you've already got, you'll walk away and expect nothing further? And you'll break things off with Jess and never contact her again?"

"No," she says. "The $1.2 million I already have doesn't enter into it."

"You're saying you expect to get $6.2 million out of this?"

"It's a small price to pay to keep me out of your life, Alison. And Jessie's."

I sigh. "Okay."

Her face registers surprise. "You'll pay me the five million?"

"No. I'll agree to your first deal: I'll pay you the two million and you can date Jessie when she turns sixteen."

Chapter 14

NICKI'S EYES GROW wide. "So you *are* willing to sell your daughter!"

"Don't be absurd. I'm just being practical. Like you said, if I refuse to let her see you, she'll sneak out behind my back anyway, and when I find out, we'll fight, I'll punish her, and she'll resent me. The harder I try to keep you apart the more she'll want to see you. But you know what? Jessie's smart. If I let her see you, no strings attached, she'll come to the conclusion she's more in love with the *idea* of you than being with you." She pauses. "But I do have one condition: my blessing will be contingent on Jessie agreeing to finish high school."

"That's it?"

"What else *is* there? It's not like I'll have any control when she turns eighteen. She'll have her inheritance and will probably wind up a bum."

"I have to say I'm surprised you'd offer Jessie up like this."

"I gave you my reasons, but here's another: I despise what you're doing, but if you're willing to give up $3 million just to date her, your feelings must be genuine. And given the choice between dating you or getting knocked up by some pimply asshole who doesn't give a shit about her, I'll choose you in a heartbeat."

Nicki studies me for several seconds. Then says, "I see what you're up to."

"What's that?"

"You're gonna give me and Jess enough rope to hang ourselves."

"That's a particularly ugly and thoughtless comment."

"Personally, I thought it was clever, and apt as hell. Because I think you intend to hire a private detective to catch us in the act. Then you'll give the evidence to the police, and with any luck, I'll go to prison."

"Not true, Nicki. I'm being completely sincere."

"There's a way to prove it."

"I'm listening."

"Go to court and have Jess emancipated. Furnish a written statement saying she has your permission to live with me after she turns sixteen."

"Live with you?"

"Just when school's out: summers, fall break, winter break..."

"If I do that, you'll keep your mouth shut?"

"I will if you will."

"Michael can't know about this. I mean, about you."

"Of course not. But he's also not going to approve of me banging his sister, so you'll have to find a way to keep him from harassing us."

"Any suggestions?"

"No. And I'd say you've got an uphill battle."

"I agree. But just to be clear: if Jessie changes her mind at any point and wants to end the relationship you'll abide by the terms of our agreement?"

"Absolutely. I must say, you're putting a lot of trust in Jessie to change her mind about loving me."

"It's simple math, Nicki. She's fifteen, and you're what, twenty-two?"

"Twenty-three."

"She'll change her mind. And if I'm wrong, at least I'll know she's happy."

"What about holidays?" Nicki says.

"What do you mean?"

"Jess won't know who I am and she won't know about our agreement. She loves me, remember? She'll expect me to visit from time to time during the school year. Not to mention Christmas, birthdays, cookouts, other family events."

"Surely you don't expect Michael and me to—"

"I don't see how you'll be able to keep her from inviting me. Or how I'll be able to refuse her invitations. Remember, your agreement with her—other than attending high school—is no-strings."

I think about that, then take a deep breath. "Okay, you win. I'll pay the five million."

"It's insignificant compared to the estate," she says.

I can see it on Nicki's face: she thinks she kicked my ass just now. Yes, we went around and around, and in the end I paid her full price. But she didn't beat me, I was willing to pay her five million from the start. But David taught me long ago that people like to haggle, and like to walk away from a negotiation thinking they got the better end of the deal. Nicki's right: $5 million *is* a pittance relative to David's estate, but I still wanted to make her work for it. Now that she's happy with the deal she struck, she'll get the hell out of our lives once and for all, and I saved a ton of money. Because this will not only keep Nicki's hands off Jessie's *body*, but also her inheritance. So good riddance, Nicki Hill. I hope you die a horrible death.

Part Three:

David Thorne

Chapter 1

Yesterday Morning

COULD THERE BE anything more humiliating than having Alison come home two hours from now to find me naked, swinging from a rope, covered in ejaculate, after masturbating to babysitter porn?

If there is, I can't think of it.

But apart from mortifying the shit out of her, which she deserves, I'm practically guaranteeing my family will get an extra $7 million from my various accidental death policies and double indemnity life riders if I happen to die.

My only concern is the embarrassment this type of death would cause Jessie. Thankfully, she won't have to see me like that, since Alison will shield her from the view. But it's bound to have an effect on her, especially at school, where whispers and rumors will run rampant. But apart from the monetary benefit, I'd justify it this way: one, it will make Jessie stronger. Two, high school kids get bored quickly, and within months my death will be old news. Three, this is a rock-star way to die, and since you never know how her age group will react to scandal, she's just as apt to become famous from it. Maybe she'll be the next Kardashian.

Of course, that's *if* I die, which is worst-case scenario.

While tying the slip knot, I can't help but think about Nicki, and how things got to this point:

Chapter 2

In Retrospect

IN RETROSPECT, I realize Nicki was setting me up from the very first visit. You know how some teenage girls—like Jessie's friend Holly—are natural flirts? Give these young ones three years to perfect their craft, and by 18 they're accomplished prick-teasers. From there, a scant few will continue practicing what works, discarding what doesn't, until they've elevated flirting to an art form.

Start there, add fashion sense, personality, and stunning beauty, and you'll approximate the Nicki Hill I met fifteen months ago. I didn't realize it at the time, but I was a sitting duck, waiting to have my feathers plucked.

For me, it was all about Michael that first day, and I was so excited for him I somehow overlooked or dismissed what I now realize was her concerted effort to win me over. Looking back on our interactions now, it seems so obvious: she hugged me enthusiastically the day we met and hugged me hello and goodbye every time thereafter. These weren't friendly, innocent side-ways hugs, but full-frontal ones that included pressing her body into mine just enough for me to experience

116

the swell of her breasts, engage with the scent of her cologne, and appreciate her signature move of holding the hug a full second longer than necessary.

Whenever I caught her staring at me she'd widen her eyes as if asking if there's something I wanted to say. Whenever I spoke she paid rapt attention, making me feel special, important, and *interesting*.

They say married men fantasize about having affairs with gorgeous women, but the meaningful, lasting affairs require women who shower them with the attention and affection they can no longer get from their wives. Beauty apart, Nicki exuded empathy and the desire to care for others. I saw it in the way she was attentive to Michael, and in the way she gave me total respect and hung on my every word. I saw it in the way she asked Alison about cooking and social graces, and especially in the way she insisted on having in-the-room, behind-the-door alone time with Jessie whenever she came to visit.

From all appearances, Nicki was the perfect woman.

And when she pounced, I never saw it coming.

Chapter 3

First Visit

MICHAEL AND NICKI are here for the weekend, their third visit, and I feel like an idiot admitting this, but before they arrived I looked out the window several times hoping to catch sight of her. It's been a month since I've seen her and I wanted to watch her exit the car, see what she's wearing, wanted to note her expression as she approached the door. At the risk of sounding like a voyeur, I love staring at her when she's unaware, and enjoy seeing her move through the world even as I try to picture what it would be like to wake up beside her.

Nicki arrived at our doorstep on Michael's arm late last August, and we sat on the kitchen barstools for a solid hour getting to know her before Alison said, "We thought we'd barbecue tonight, if that's okay with you."

"I'd love that!" Nicki said.

"Plenty of time for a swim, if you're interested. Did you bring a suit?"

"I did," she said, and boy, did she!

Alison saw her first, and abruptly located me in the kitchen and said, "Try not to step on your tongue when you see her."

"Who?"

She frowned and walked outside, and I couldn't get out to the patio fast enough. Knowing Alison was eyeing me like a hawk, I didn't get to leer, but I saw what I needed to see. Jessie saw it too and abruptly announced, "I'm never eating ice cream again!"

That weekend Nicki was the perfect guest. She was up for anything, never lost her smile, insisted on pitching in, and took a genuine interest in our family, learning our hobbies and what each of us considered important in our lives. And she accomplished all this without giving the impression she was sucking up or trying too hard to make a good impression. Though she found a way to give us all quality time, including Michael, she spent more time with Jessie than anyone else, and—crazy as it sounds—we could see Jessie transforming into a better kid hour by hour.

By Saturday night Jessie's patented eye-rolling, sullen attitude, and snarky comments had vanished. She was sitting up straight, dressing well, carrying herself with poise, talking to us as if she genuinely cared what we were saying.

On Sunday morning Alison was annoyed she had to call the girls to breakfast three times, but when they finally came bounding into the kitchen giggling like eight-year-olds, Nicki announced: "Come see what we've done!" They led us up the stairs to Jessie's room, opened the door, and left us standing with gaping mouths: they'd gotten up at the crack of dawn and spent hours rearranging Jessie's furniture and cleaning her room from top to bottom.

And it looked like something out of a magazine.

Alison said, "Jessie, my God! Your room didn't look this good the day we moved in!"

Jessie beamed, but gave credit where credit was due: "It was Nicki's vision," she said.

"Well, whatever inspired it," Alison said, "we've got our daughter back."

And that was just the first weekend!

Chapter 4

Breakups, Makeups, and

SPECIAL OCCASIONS

I LOVE MY son, but watching him and Nicki together I always got the sense they were mismatched, as if she was the parent, and he was the child. Unlike most young lovers, they didn't appear to be overly sexual. While always attentive, I never saw Nicki initiate the caressing. What I *did* notice, she seemed to slightly stiffen whenever he put his arm around her or drew her in for a kiss. Michael has never spoken to me about their relationship, but according to Alison, they'd been having problems.

"Like what?" I asked.

"He says she's moody, cold, and emotionally unavailable."

"What does that *mean:* emotionally unavailable?"

"I think it's his way of saying she's asexual."

"A sexual what?"

She gave me a look. "Are you trying to make a *joke?*"

"Oh. You mean—"

"Michael didn't *say* it, but I get the impression she has no interest in sex."

"That's awfully hard to believe!"

"It is?" she said. "Why?"

"I just meant—"

"Don't bother," she said. "I know *exactly* what you meant."

That afternoon the old Jessie showed up sullen, angry, and unkempt. When I asked what was wrong she said, "Michael's an asshole."

"He called?"

"*She* did."

"*Nicki* called you?"

Jessie showed me an ugly look. "Why is *that* so hard to believe? We talk all the time."

"You *do*?" Alison said. "About what?"

Jessie suddenly looked defensive. "I didn't mean we talk *all* the time. I don't *bother* her, or anything like that. We probably talk a few minutes every other week."

I said, "Why's Michael being an asshole?"

"They had another fight. She left him."

Alison said, "I wouldn't worry. From what I gather it happens all the time. And she always comes back."

"One day she won't," Jessie said. "And we'll never see her again."

"You sound more upset about it than Michael."

Jessie gave her mom a withering look, then stormed out of the room.

"Maybe it's best they finally break up for good," Alison said. "She's affecting both our kids."

I said, "Personally, I like Jessie better when Nicki and Michael are getting along."

"Me too."

John Locke

Of course, Michael turned out to be right: Nicki came back. We didn't see her on Labor Day, due to the breakup, but she was back in time for Alison's birthday in October, and she and Michael spent Thanksgiving with us, and Christmas, and then—surprise—another breakup, but—bigger surprise, Nicki showed up for Jessie's birthday anyway, which delighted Jessie more than all her gifts combined. That was late January. By Valentine's Day she and Michael were back together, and visited us the following week. And every time she showed up, it had a positive impact on our family, especially Jessie. Our inside joke was as long as Michael and Nicki are together, Alison and I get to live with Good Jessie.

Chapter 5

First Move

IF I HAD to pick the exact date and time Nicki made her first move on me I'd say Christmas morning, as the family opened presents. She bought Jessie some sort of miniature Bluetooth music player and pre-loaded it with all sorts of dreadful music that turned out to be Jessie's favorite artists. When Nicki named some of the people, I was the only one in the room who didn't know them. Naturally, this gave the whole family the opportunity to make fun of Old David and my "ancient" taste in music. As they ribbed me I noticed Nicki was smiling politely, but didn't join in. And when Alison made a snide remark about my favorite band: "You'll have to forgive him, Nicki. David's idea of great music is *Rush*, which happens to be the number one most hated band in the history of music!" —Nicki's smile faded, and she said: "Actually, I like *Rush*." Then she looked directly into my eyes and said, "Especially *Double Agent*."

To most people, that remark wouldn't remotely be considered "making a move on David." But the fact she publicly stood up for me after my *wife's* insult...well, that got my attention.

124

Had it stopped there, I wouldn't have considered it excessive flirtation. But the next night while waiting for everyone to get dressed to go out to dinner, I was sitting alone in the den, enjoying a drink. To my utter shock Nicki came up behind me, kissed my cheek and whispered, "You look amazing, David!"

Her words and kiss played in my mind day and night for weeks. That night at dinner I tried to avoid looking at her, but couldn't help myself. At one point she and Jessie got up to use the bathroom and when they reentered the room Nicki gave me a perfect wink. In other words, when she closed her right eye nothing else moved. Not her jaw, her nose, her cheek...it was practiced, perfect, and it conveyed a distinct message.

That night, lying in bed, I replayed it over and over in my mind. She stuck up for me against Alison. She kissed my cheek. She said I looked amazing. She winked at me. It was enough on its own, but when I replayed it the tenth or twelfth time, it hit me: she loved the song *Double Agent*.

Leaving nothing to chance, I grabbed my phone, looked up the definition, and came up with this:

Double Agent: *a person who pretends to work for one side,*
while secretly working for the other.

I wondered if Nicki was smart enough to pass me a message based on her knowledge of my musical taste, and decided she probably was. That's what double agents do: they pass messages to the side they're truly working for. She knew back in August my all-time favorite band was *Rush*. Favorite groups was one of the first questions she asked me. So she had plenty of time to come up with the song.

But was I reading too much into this? Could the song have been a coincidence? I hoped not, because I didn't have to work too hard to read between the lines and deduce she was really saying as a double agent she was pretending to be with Michael while secretly wanting to be with me.

Chapter 6

Second Move

IF CHRISTMAS WAS her first move, her second came in late January, at Jessie's birthday party. Jessie reveled in showing off Nicki to her friends, and once again Nicki came up with the perfect gift: Taylor Swift concert tickets. Jessie asked Nicki to take her.

"Are you sure?" Nicki said.

"Yes! One hundred percent! Please say yes. *Please!*"

"Okay, then: yes!"

After giving her a big hug, Jessie said, "Come with us to the theater room. We're gonna watch *Kardashian* reruns!"

"I really didn't come here to crash your party," Nicki said, "but if you're seriously inviting me—"

"I am! You *have* to! It'll be so much fun!"

"In that case...absolutely!"

Alison said, "Jess, I need to talk to Nicki a second."

Jessie gave her a look, but Nicki said, "I'll be right there."

As Jess and her friends raced to claim their seats, Alison said, "Michael's on his way."

Nicki's face fell. "I should go. I don't want to cause any drama."

"I know he'd love to see you."

"Last time we talked, he said he wasn't coming."

"I think the only reason he's coming is to see you."

"How did he even know I'm here?"

"Jessie told him. He called to wish her happy birthday and she told him to hurry if he wanted to see you. She said she'd keep you here till he arrives."

Nicki smiled. "That little scamp!"

Alison said, "I thought you should know. I didn't want to put you in an awkward situation."

"I wouldn't want it to take away from Jess's party."

"It was her idea. She's afraid if you and Michael break up she'll never see you again."

"That's so sweet."

"She loves you. We all do."

"Well, okay then. I'll stay. Thanks for telling me."

I watched all this take place while clearing the dining room table as Alison rinsed the dishes. Then Alison asked me to cut the cookie cake, so I started that task and Nicki began arranging the pieces on a giant platter. Alison grabbed a bunch of plates and forks and said, "How many pieces are you up to?"

Nicki did a quick count. "Twenty."

"That's plenty. Can you bring the platter on your way to the theater room?"

"Of course."

When Alison left the room Nicki picked up the platter, looked me dead in the eyes and said, "How about you, David? Do *you* want a piece?"

My first thought was: *Omigod! She has no idea what she just said!* But her knowing smile implied she knew exactly what she said.

"Um...are we talking about the cookie cake?"

"Is that what you *want* to talk about? The cookie cake?"

"Not necessarily."

"You know what *I* think?"

"Tell me."

"We need to talk. Bigtime."

"I'd like that."

"Yes," she said. "I'm *positive* you will."

Then she sighed, gave me a wistful look, and took the tray downstairs.

Chapter 7

Third Move

NICKI AND MICHAEL were back together again in February, and he brought her to see us for an overnight visit. I couldn't help notice she was avoiding me, acting quite cold toward me. We only got one chance alone, and that lasted 30 seconds.

I said, "Is everything all right?"

"Is it?" she said.

"You seem upset."

"You think?"

"What's wrong?"

"I'm with Michael."

"I noticed that."

"You never called."

"What?"

She turned and walked away.

Chapter 8

Fourth Move

NICKI SPENT MOST of her March visit hanging out with Jessie. They went shopping, went to a movie, worked on a music project together, and Nicki even let her practice driving her car up and down our driveway. Meanwhile, Michael and I played golf on Saturday and Sunday and he and his mom spent the evenings chatting while waiting for Nicki to get tired of hanging out with Jessie.

Although Nicki barely spoke to me Saturday and Sunday, on Friday night she caught me alone, gave me a thumbs up and whispered, "If we ever go out on a date, that's the outfit I want you to wear, okay?"

I smiled.

"Don't forget," she said.

Chapter 9

April 15th

The Phone Call

NICKI'S APRIL BREAKUP with Michael appeared to be far more serious than previous ones. She not only moved out of his apartment, but took all her things with her and rented a small old house in Shelbyville, Kentucky, which is about 30 miles closer to Lexington. After three days of not hearing from her, Michael panicked and began calling. When Nicki failed to answer he realized he had no idea where she had moved. So he called Jessie and asked if she'd heard from Nicki.

She hadn't.

He asked her to call Nicki to make sure she was okay. When Jessie did, Nicki answered and seemed perfectly normal, laughing and joking. At one point Nicki asked: "Does he honestly think I can't survive without him?" And Jessie said, "That's how he made it sound."

"Tell him I'm fine."

"He wants to know where you're staying."

"I'm sure he does. But I'd prefer not to see him."

"Can I at least tell him what state you're in?"

"Colorado."

"Omigod! Is that *true?*"

"Not even!"

They laughed like nothing had changed.

But Michael wasn't laughing. He couldn't believe she'd finally moved on, and wasn't ready to accept it. He asked Alison to intervene, and so she called Nicki to see if she'd come to the house to talk about it. Nicki surprised her by showing up, and after what Alison considered a "very promising talk" Nicki spent the better part of the afternoon hanging out with Jessie, and reassuring her that no matter what happened between her and Michael, they'd remain friends. As proof, Nicki pointed out she hadn't forgotten her promise to take Jessie to the concert which was still months away.

Since I wasn't home when Nicki spoke to Alison she asked if she could call me, to get my perspective on how Michael might view their future. Alison thought that was a good idea, and that evening she sat me down and explained that Nicki had serious psycho-sexual issues resulting from horrendous childhood experiences with foster fathers, and apparently certain foster kids as well.

"You should convince her to get counseling," Alison said.

"I'll try."

"That girl's got serious issues, David. I wonder if I did the right thing, encouraging her to get back together with Michael. All afternoon I worried about it and wondered if maybe this breakup could be the best thing that ever happened to him."

"It would break his heart," I said.

"True, but...she's never going to want children and they're always going to have bedroom issues. I'm not sure she's right for Michael."

Several days passed before Nicki finally called, and when she did, I almost didn't answer because I didn't recognize the number.

"David?"

"Yes?"

"It's Nicki."

"Nicki!" I said, with far too much enthusiasm. "How are you?"

"Dazed." She made a small laugh. "Are you confused?" She added, "By the way, that's a movie reference."

"Right."

"You have no clue which movie I'm talking about, do you?"

"Uh...no. Sorry."

"Never mind. It was a stupid reference. Are you at work?"

"I am."

"In the middle of something, or is this a good time to talk?"

"No. I mean, yes, I can talk. Absolutely!"

She laughed. "You sound unsure of what to say. Can I make a suggestion?"

"Please do."

"Relax. To answer your question truthfully, I'm fine. In fact, I've never been better."

"That's..."

"Yes?"

"I was getting ready to say that's great, but I'm not sure where things stand with you and Michael. According to Alison, you're considering getting back together."

She paused. "Is that what *you* want?"

I paused.

She said, "David? Is that what you hope happens? That Michael and I get back together?"

"I...I guess I want what's best for everyone."

"Well, that could be a problem, because in my experience it's impossible to please everyone."

"That's true."

"I'd like to tell you about a decision I've made: for the first time ever, I want to do what's best for me. Does that sound selfish?"

"No, of course not," I said. "You deserve to be happy."

"I agree. Do you remember what I said to you at Jessie's birthday party? I said we needed to talk. Do you remember what you said?"

"I said I'd like that."

"Exactly. And I was hoping you'd call me."

"I realized that much later."

"I know. I brought it to your attention. And yet you still didn't call."

"You'd gone back with Michael. I wasn't sure the offer still applied."

"It did. And...it still does. Would it put you in an awkward situation or make you feel uncomfortable if I asked you to meet me someplace so we can finally have that talk in person?"

The angel on my shoulder said: *Absolutely not! It wouldn't be appropriate.*

But the devil on my other shoulder said: *This is Nicki Hill, the goddess you've blistered your dick fantasizing about for the past eight months.*

The angel said: *Your son loves this woman with all his heart and whatever you say next will have major implications on your future and everyone you love. Do the right thing, David: don't disappoint God.*

After weighing both sides of the argument I said, "I'd be thrilled to meet you, Nicki. When and where?"

Scum that I am, my mind was in overdrive, hoping she'd name a hotel. On the one hand, that would be the most exciting thing that's happened to me in a decade. On the other, I'd probably explode in my pants before I got past the lobby, and wouldn't *that* be emasculating! As it turned out, she named a little sandwich shop on the other side of town and asked, "Have you ever been there?"

I hadn't.

"It's near the Griffin Gate Marriott, by the Interstate."

"Right. That should be easy to find."

"I don't know if the food's any good," she said. "I was just thinking of a safe place we could meet where you're not likely to run into anyone you know."

"It's a good choice. When do you want to meet?"

"I know it's awfully short notice, but…would today work? Around noon?"

"Actually, yes. That's perfect." I checked my watch. "Can you get there that quickly?"

"If not, will you wait for me?"

"Of course."

"How long?"

"As long as it takes."

"Thanks, David. Because that's how long I've been waiting for you."

Wow! Did she just say that?

She did.

So I said, "I'm honored."

And it was the truth.

She said, "Call me back at this number when you get to the parking lot. If it's real busy I've got a backup plan."

"Will do."

Chapter 10

First Date

WHEN I PULLED into the parking lot I was a bit concerned by the large number of cars. I'm not famous, but I *am* fairly well-known in Lexington, and it could cause problems if one of Alison's friends happened to see me there with Nicki.

I called to give her the news.

"I thought that might be the case," she said.

"What's your backup plan?"

"If I tell you, will you promise not to get the wrong impression?"

"Yes. Absolutely."

"I'm at the Griffin Gate Marriott. Room 214."

"Cool."

"We're just going to talk, okay?"

"No problem," I said, thinking just the two of us in a hotel room beats a crowded restaurant any day.

She said, "I'll leave the door slightly ajar so you won't have to knock. That might call attention to yourself."

"Good point. Should I come right now?"

"Please. I've already ordered room service."

I drove to the hotel, parked my car in a cluster of others, thinking it would be less conspicuous, then moved through the hotel lobby as quickly as possible. Entering the elevator, it dawned on me I was acting like a man about to cheat on his wife. I suppose that's because in my mind, I already *was*.

But Nicki made it perfectly clear this meeting was just going to be a talk. She ordered room service for the occasion. So it's not cheating.

When I got to the second floor I exited the elevator, walked to the room, pushed the door open, closed it behind me.

One part of my brain thought the whole "talk and room service" comments might be a ploy, and I'd go in and find her lying on the bed in a negligee, or better yet, naked under the covers. But the truth was far less racy. The room was actually a suite, and the door I entered led to the couch and table, not the bedroom.

Nor was Nicki naked or wearing a negligee. She was wearing black, skin-tight yoga pants and a crop top, and oversized white Nike Dunk Sky High sneakers with the laces untied. It was a simple look that came across sexy as hell. When she saw me she jumped to her feet and raced across the room to greet me.

I didn't know how to react: should I start the hug? Wait for one? Was she going to kiss me? If so, should I kiss her back?

She hugged me, and as usual, held it longer than friends would.

Much longer.

When at last she backed away, she had tears in her eyes.

"What's wrong?" I said.

"I'm just...so *happy!*"

"Me too, Nicki."

We made small talk till the food arrived, then we ate and talked some more. Neither of us mentioned Michael or Alison, though we did talk about Jessie, and her friends, and the upcoming concert.

When the talk died down Nicki said, "Let's move to the sofa." Once there, she said, "So David."

"Yes?"

She blushed, placed her hand on my thigh. "Are you going to make me say it out loud?"

"I'm afraid so."

"Very well. I want to be your mistress. If you'll have me."

I nearly choked. "What about Michael?"

"He'll have to find his own mistress."

Chapter 11

"SO WHAT DO you think?" she said.

"That's the most amazing thing I've ever heard. How would it work?"

"Excuse me?"

"I mean, the logistics. The ground rules. The end game."

"End game?"

"You said mistress, and I couldn't possibly be more excited. I was just wondering if you're thinking it might lead to something more."

"Like what?"

"Marriage."

"You're already married."

"Well...yes. What I mean is, I wouldn't rule anything out where you're concerned. I've been fantasizing about you for months. I was just wondering how far you felt this could—"

"David?"

"Yes?"

"Let's not put the cart before the horse."

"Okay."

"How about we start with a checklist. Do you find me attractive?"

"God, yes!"

"Check. Do you find me desirable?"

"Incredibly so."

"Check. Do you trust me?"

"Yes."

"How much?"

"Completely."

"Check. Here's the big one: I'm not sure what you may have heard about...my background. But if we're going to do this, it has to be at my pace, or it's gonna go badly. Can you be patient with me?"

"Absolutely."

"Are you willing to go at my pace?"

"Yes. If at any point you're not comfortable with whatever's happening, just—"

She shook her head. "That won't be a problem because you're going to let things develop at my pace."

"Of course."

"This isn't going to be about fucking."

"It's not?"

"It's gonna be about making love."

"I'm with you 100%!"

She studied my face before saying, "I'm aching to make love to you. But you know what? Anyone can have sex. Dogs and cats can have sex. I hope you can rise above that and be patient and allow the sexual tension to grow more and more powerful each time we see each other."

"I'm open to whatever works for you."

"You won't be sorry, David. I'm worth waiting for. I'll be the best lover you ever had."

"I believe you. Um...how long do you think we'll be putting off the uh..."

"The sex part?"

I nodded.

"We're not going to put it off at all."

"Okay."

"I'm confusing you."

"Not at all. Well, a little. But seriously Nicki, however you want to do this, I'm with you. I'm just so honored you chose me."

"Thank you. What I mean is, we're going to do something sexual every time we meet. It's just that we're not going to go all the way the first few visits. Will that work for you?"

"Yes."

"One last thing: if we're gonna do this, you'll have to promise something."

"Name it."

"You can't ever ask or tell me to do something sexual. In other words, I'll have specific plans for each time we meet. Maybe one plan is we lie in bed naked, without touching. If that's the plan, I have to be able to trust you completely."

"I understand."

"I'm serious, David. If that's the plan you absolutely can't touch me. Because if that's the plan and you do, you'll never see me again."

I cocked my head, wondering two things: first: is this what happened over and over with her and Michael? And second: is she just plain crazy?

But it didn't matter. By then I was in striking distance of epic pussy, and I'd have said yes to anything.

And so I did.

"Check," she said. Then added, "I like what you said a while ago about logistics and ground rules. I have some ideas on that, if you'd like to hear them."

"I'd love to."

Chapter 12

"FIRST," SHE SAID, "I want us to talk about Michael and Alison. I want us to tell and ask each other everything we'd like to say and know about them. And we have to be 100% honest. In other words, if I ask if you love Alison and you do, I'll think no less of you, and it won't affect our relationship in the least. Because what we do in *this* world is separate from what you do in *that* world. But if you lie in order to justify our relationship, or because you think it's what I want to hear, I'll know. And if that's the case, you're not the man I hoped for, and that will end it. So always tell the truth, because I'll accept nothing less."

"I'll always be honest with you. You have my word."

She paused. "So we'll talk about Michael and Alison till there's nothing left to say. But just today. After you leave the room today, whenever we're together, we can never mention either of them, ever again. Agreed?"

I nodded.

"Second, when it's over, it's over."

"Okay. Uh...can you expand on that a little?"

"If for any reason you change your mind about being with me—"

"That will never happen!"

"I hope not. But maybe you will someday, or maybe I'll want to end things. If either of us wants to, the other has to accept it. This is a problem I've had with Michael, and I kept going back time and time again, and you know why?"

I shook my head. I've never understood that. Maybe she just can't say no.

She said, "It's because of you. I felt you were worth fighting for. And believe me, Michael and I fought a lot."

"Are you saying you stayed with him to—"

"That's right. Just to get *you*. I knew I wanted you the moment we met. And I hung in there, month after month, waiting for my next opportunity to try to get you interested in me."

"That's why you kept hoping I'd call."

"Exactly. And that's why I was angry when you didn't. Because I had to stay with him until the next chance to be around you. It was torture, David."

"I can see that now. I'm so sorry."

"Third," she said, "I'm going to do things with you sexually that I've never done with anyone else. Things I've never *wanted* to do with anyone else. But as they happen, I don't want you to ask if I've ever done these things before, and especially with Michael, because I did not. I'll tell you more about that when we talk about him."

"I'm very excited about everything you've said, Nicki. I can't wait."

"Good. Me either. Fourth: we can never text each other. We'll set up a specific time each week, and you'll call me as close to that time as you can. If for some reason you can't call, do *not* leave a message. This is for your protection more than mine. Fifth: I will never call you. There are too many things that could go wrong in your life if I do."

"What if I call at the appointed time and you don't answer? Should I wait a few minutes and call back?"

"No. If I don't answer the first time you call, it's because I can't. We'll just have to miss that week."

"That would be awful."

"I agree. So let's both do our best."

"Sounds good."

"I only have one more, and it's different than the others. I want to ask you a question, and I want you to answer it as honestly as you can."

"Ask it."

"How does it make you feel to know you're gonna get in my pants?"

I closed my eyes. "Like I'm in heaven. Like I won the Powerball. Like my whole life was building up to this." I opened my eyes and looked at her, and I swear, I had tears in my eyes as I said, "I will never let you down. I only hope I don't disappoint you."

"Number six is never forget how you're feeling this very moment. Things will happen, David. Situations. Problems. At some point I might do something or say something that makes you furious. But if that happens, I want you to always remember exactly how you're feeling right now."

"I promise I will. Can I kiss you now? I'm dying to—"

Pow!

What the *fuck*?

She slapped me harder than I've ever been slapped in my life. Then she said, "Were you not listening this whole time? Did I not say you can't ask me to do anything sexual?"

"You did. I'm so sorry. I didn't realize—"

—What I didn't realize is she was bat shit crazy!

"It's okay," she said. "I was planning to kiss you in a little while anyway. It's just..." she sighed, looked away.

"I know. I'm sorry. It won't happen again."

She took a full minute to compose herself, then said, "How much time do you have?"

"For you, all the time in the world."

She smiled. "Good. Let's get this last order of business out of the way: our talk about Michael and Alison. Want me to start?"

"Please."

"Here's my baggage with Michael: I know he's your son and my biggest worry is you're going to think about him and me being together when you and I are together. And that would totally suck. So that's why I have to tell you something that shames me to my core to admit: I never loved Michael. And—I'm just being honest now, because that's the promise we made—I basically used him to get you interested. I've been the worst girlfriend in the world. I gave him the least affection possible, and if you have specific questions about what we did sexually that I fail to cover, I'll answer truthfully, but just until you leave this room today. So anyway—and this is the truth—I've never given him oral, and in all the months we've been together we've had intercourse exactly twice. Both times lasted about 30 seconds, and afterward I threw up."

"You threw up both times?"

She nodded.

"Why do you think that happened?"

"This is really painful to tell you because I can't do it without getting mental pictures. But I owe you an explanation, so the plain truth is Michael reminds me of the worst thing that happened in my past. It's not his fault, it's a combination of things: the way he whispers when he's coming on to me? The way he touches me? His sexual mannerisms? I don't know. Could be all of these, could be something else. It's like a mental block. I tried to overcome it lots of times, but I couldn't. So of course he thinks I have deep-seated psycho-sexual issues, and I suppose I do where he's concerned. I've always felt badly about it, but...what can I do? I simply never found him physically appealing. He's touched me, but only a few times below the waist. And whenever he did that, or tried to, I got upset and broke up with him. Then, because of you, I came back. In the interest of full disclosure, I should add I used my hand to make him excited numerous times over the past year, to keep the peace. Do you understand what I mean by that?"

I nodded.

She said, "We weren't really engaged. I agreed to let him tell people that—especially you, Alison and Jessie—so you wouldn't keep pressuring him. You probably know Michael has a temper. He's never hit me or anything, but he's verbally abusive. You don't have to agree, or comment, that's just my opinion. And even though I never cheated on him, he always accused me of it. I think that's mostly my fault, since I wouldn't let him touch me. Is there anything you'd like to ask me about Michael or our relationship?"

I thought about everything she said before answering "No."

"Are you sure?"

"I am. You covered it very well."

"Do you think you can forgive me for the way I treated him?"

"There's no need. You tried to make it work and Michael accepted the relationship you were able to give him, just as I will."

"Can you keep from thinking about him and me when you and I are together?"

"Like you said, Nicki: what happens here is totally apart from what happens elsewhere."

She smiled. "Thank you, David. I was certain you'd understand. There's just one more thing."

"What's that?"

Chapter 13

"IN A MOMENT of weakness, I let Michael talk me into taking nude pictures of me. They're on his phone. The reason I'm bringing this up is, Michael has a temper, and sometimes he's verbally abusive. He said if I don't come back to him he's going to put my photos on a revenge site."

"What's that?"

"Do you ever watch porn?"

"No."

"Well, there are porn sites where guys punish their ex-wives or girlfriends by posting their nude photos. Then the porn sites sell them to other porn sites and within days the photos are all over the world and there's nothing the women can do about it."

"That's horrible. I'm sure Michael didn't mean it."

"Maybe not, but I can't take that chance."

"Is there anything I can do?"

"If you can get your hands on his phone you could erase them."

I frowned. "I'm not very skilled with cell phones."

"I can show you how. It's super easy."

"You want to show me now?"

"No. Because in order to delete the photos, you'll have to see them. And I'm not quite ready for that."

I nodded. "Well, whenever you're ready, show me what to do and I'll make it happen."

"Thank you."

"Can I ask *you* a question, Nicki? You said you'll always have a plan for what we're going to do each time we get together. Are you going to tell me the plan each week when I call you?"

"No, and please don't ask. I want it to be a surprise."

"No problem. I like surprises."

"But if my plan is something you don't feel like doing, you can say no. But that would probably set our relationship back instead of moving it forward."

"Well, I wouldn't want that to happen. Um...just to be clear, we're not talking about bondage, are we? Or domination?"

"*Omigod, no!* Is that okay?"

"Absolutely."

"Good, because I'm totally not into those sorts of things."

"Me either!"

"Let's move on. Is there anything else you'd like to ask or talk about, as far as the ground rules?"

"Not really. I think you've covered everything."

"Nothing more on Michael?"

"Nope."

"Okay, then let's talk about Alison. Your turn to start."

Chapter 14

I TOOK A minute to think about how to condense a twenty-five-year marital relationship into a couple of sentences, and came up with: "I do love Alison, but we sleep in separate beds when you guys aren't visiting. She's not a romantic person, and I think she probably loves me in general, but certainly not like she used to. We've never cheated on each other, but I've come close a couple of times."

"What stopped you?"

"I never met anyone I'd be willing to lose my marriage over. At least, not until you came along."

"You're willing to lose Alison over me?"

"Yes."

"Thank you. That's quite a compliment."

"You're welcome. So anyway, we've done a lot of settling in our marriage over the years and probably would have divorced by now, had it not been for Jessie. It'll be interesting to see what happens when she goes off to college."

"How often do you make love?"

Before I can answer, she says, "Remember, you have to tell the truth."

"I will. Let me think a minute. It varies. She's really weird about sex."

"How so?"

"She only wants to do it when we're out of town, which is rare. But over the past few years she hasn't even wanted to do it then."

"When was the last time you made love to her?"

"This is going to sound weird, but...we did it last week."

"*What?*"

"Before that it's been at least two years."

"What happened last week?"

"You came to visit. Alison told me you were going to call me. I guilted her into having sex."

"Did she know you were thinking about me the whole time?"

"I think so. She certainly accused me of it afterward."

Nicki giggled. "Poor Alison. Tell me more about her."

"There's really not much to tell. We're coexisting. We're roommates, not lovers."

"She's very pretty."

"She is."

"What does she look like naked?"

"Excuse me?"

"Remember our agreement? We can ask *anything*. And the other person has to answer truthfully."

"She looks good."

"Details."

"You've seen her."

"Not naked."

"Right. Well, her breasts are average, I'd say, and they're spread a little wider than average." I looked at her and laughed. "You want more details?"

She nodded.

"You mean like her nipples?"

"Tell me everything."

"Well, they're average, I guess. More pink than brown, and they're surprisingly long when erect. Her tits don't really sag, like you'd expect."

"She's only forty, David."

"Right. What I mean is they're quite firm for her age, I think."

"Does she shave her bush?"

"Whoa. Uh...no. She trims it."

"Every day?"

"I think so."

"What's her natural hair color?"

"Same as her eyebrows."

"Did you ever give her anal?"

"*Anal? ...Alison?*" I laughed. "No way!"

"Does she pleasure herself at night?"

"I don't know."

"Have you ever caught her doing it?"

"Once. A long time ago."

"Did she use her hand, or—"

"She was lying on her back in the bathtub with her legs spread apart, straight up in the air. She was letting the water do the work."

"You came up on her unannounced?"

"Exactly."

"Was she embarrassed?"

"Mortified."

"How'd she react?"

"She was furious."

"With you?"

I nodded.

"That's so typical. I'm sorry."

"Not your fault," I said, wondering what she meant. How would she know what's typical behavior for Alison? Or maybe she meant it was a typical reaction for a 40-year-old woman. Or a wife. Or...

"Is she loud in bed when you're having sex?"

"Not these days."

"What about before?"

I laughed. "She was pretty vocal."

Nicki smiled. "Did she yell Fuck me! and stuff like that?"

"Yeah."

"Imitate her."

"For real?"

"Uh huh."

I raised my voice an octave and started hollering, "Oh God! Oh... Oh YES! Oh! Fuck me! Fuck me! FUCK me! Oh...I'm...I'm cumming! Oh God! Oh, Oh my GOD!"

By then Nicki and I were laughing hysterically.

Then she said, "You'd do her every night if you could."

"Probably."

"She still rocks your world."

"You think?"

"I know it for a fact." She pointed to my crotch. "Is that a gun in your pocket, or are you excited to see me?"

"I'm definitely excited to see you."

"And yet you chubbed up *after* describing your naked wife."

"So it would appear. Is that okay?"

"It's sad."

"In what way?"

"You want *her*, but she's fucking your insurance agent."

"She's...*What?*"

Chapter 15

"WHAT ARE YOU *talking* about?"

"Alison's been having an affair with your insurance agent. I can't remember his name."

"Arthur Blass?"

"That's it."

"Are you *sure?*"

"Certain."

"How do you know?"

"Jessie told me."

"She must be mistaken."

"I don't think so. I've got a copy of their texts."

"Whose texts?"

"Arthur and Alison's. You want to see them?"

"Yes."

"Why?"

"Are you *serious? My wife's cheating* on me?"

"Aren't you about to do the same to her?"

Good point. "Yes. At least, I hope so."

"That being the case, would you want her to know everything you and I have said today?"

"No."

"Then I'm going to ask you to forget everything Alison's doing with Arthur. I have copies of every text message they've ever exchanged, and I'll show them to you right now if you really want to see them. But I hope you'll resist the urge."

"Why?"

"Because Alison's my friend."

I wanted to ask if Alison's her friend, why would she have an affair with her husband, but that would certainly kill the mood. So I said, "I'll respect your wishes."

"Thank you, David. I'd also like you to promise not to confront her about it."

"Why?"

"I just told you: she's my friend. She's always been good to me. I love her."

Her words made so little sense I kept waiting for her to say "Just kidding." But she wasn't kidding. She's just nuts.

Then she said, "I really do love your wife, David. Craving you has nothing to do with how I feel about her."

"I understand."

"Good. Is there anything else we need to say about her?"

"No."

"In that case, I'd like you to leave the room, close the door behind you, and wait for me to open it."

"Seriously?"

As I stood to leave she said, "I know this seems silly, but it's symbolic. Like I said earlier, when you leave this room today we'll never talk about Michael or Alison again. And when I let you in, from now on, everything's gonna be about you and me."

"Sounds great."

I walked out the door, closed it behind me, and waited. Ten seconds later she opened the door, motioned me in, closed the door behind me, took my hand, and led me to the couch. Then she sat down and had me stand in front of her. Then she said, "Will you take your pants off now?"

"Excuse me?"

"It's part of today's plan. Like I said, you don't have to, but it'll set our relationship back if you don't."

"What's going to happen?"

"You're going to show me your penis."

"Uh...just like that?"

"Would you prefer not to? Because I think you'll be glad you did."

I kicked off my shoes, unzipped my pants, stepped out of them, stood before her.

"And the shorts and socks," she said.

"Are you—"

"What?"

"Nothing." I almost asked if she was going to remove her clothes too, but caught myself just in time. I already violated that rule once, and promised not to do it again.

Was I nervous? Of course. Self-conscious? How could I not be? I was a forty-two-year-old man getting naked in front of a goddess half my age who until two weeks ago was giving my son hand jobs on a regular basis. Although I had no idea how big Michael was, I'm sure the smart money would back him in a big dick contest. I only hoped Nicki wouldn't laugh.

As I stood before her completely naked from the waist down, I was pleased to see myself sporting the biggest erection I'd had in years. Not saying she was impressed, but at least she didn't appear disappointed.

She picked up my soggy shorts, smiled, and said: "Looks like you started without me. Can I borrow your tie?"

I removed my tie and handed it to her.

"You said you trusted me completely, David."

"I do."

She tied a slip knot into one end of my tie and put it around my neck. Then asked, "Have you ever done this before?"

"I'm not sure what we're talking about."

"Erotic asphyxiation."

"What's that?"

"The intentional restriction of oxygen to the brain for purposes of sexual arousal."

"Sounds dangerous."

"It *would* be, if you couldn't trust me. But you can. I didn't work this hard to let anything happen to you that falls short of total ecstasy."

"I like the sound of that!"

"Thank you. Stay put." She walked to the bathroom, got a face towel, and arranged it under the tie. "This will help keep it from leaving a mark," she said.

She tightened the tie until I experienced a measurable—but not considerable—degree of discomfort. In other words, I was able to breathe, but had to work for it. I'm not saying my eyes were bulging out or anything, but my neck felt exactly as you'd expect when someone puts a gentle tourniquet around it. Then she said, "Masturbate for me."

"*What?*"

"Please. For me."

"It's...I mean..."

She stood in front of me and said, "If you do, I'll take off my top."

If there's one thing I knew how to do well, this was it. So I started, and true to her word, she took off her top. To my great disappointment she was wearing a bra, but at least it was partially see-through, and I saw enough to gasp several times, and I may have even screamed.

And then it was over.

She loosened the knot, and I continued gasping for breath, and she hugged me and kissed me, and at first I couldn't kiss her back, but after a few seconds I recovered, and we rolled around on the couch and I kept telling myself: *Don't touch her! Don't ask her to do anything!*

It had already been the most amazing orgasm of my life at the point she removed the tie, then it continued for a full ten seconds afterward.

She said, "Omigod, David! You were wonderful! I'm so proud of you!"

I wasn't sure which particular part she was proud about: my erection, my stroke, my kissing...but then she showed me, and I realized she was talking about how excited I had gotten: the evidence was all over the couch as well as her pants.

"Oh, shit. I've ruined your clothes," I said. "I'm so sorry."

"Don't be silly. You were a rock star!"

And just as she predicted my mind went straight to Michael, and I wondered if she used to do this to him, and wished I'd asked her more details before leaving the room moments earlier.

Chapter 16

April-May-June-July

EVERY TUESDAY I called, and every Friday we met at noon, at different hotels. She always purchased the room, and the pattern continued: she'd give me the room number, I'd push the door open, we'd talk about everything except Michael and Alison, have something light to eat, and then she'd introduce me to her own special brand of eroticism.

With each passing week, she drew me closer and closer to the prize. The first week she led me to the bathroom and let me feel her up as she stroked me to orgasm. The second week she did the slip knot thing with my tie again, only this time she blindfolded me and made me stand on a book and told me I had to remain standing on the book at all times while she stroked me.

Obviously, I exploded.

Then, as before, she rushed to loosen the knot to keep me from passing out. After I recovered, she made me stay on the book with my blindfold on, and surprised me by removing her clothes and rubbing her body against mine from behind. Then she stepped in front of me and said, "No touching with your hands, but you can kiss them if you'd like," and so I went after her nipples like they contained the secrets of the world, and only my lips and tongue could decipher them.

Each time we met she went a little further and allowed me to experience more of her passion, more of her body, and as great as those things were—to my utter amazement—I found myself craving the tie around my neck. I loved the different things she did to make me excited, but the tie enhanced the experience beyond words. Nicki used it two weeks in a row, then skipped two weeks, and then, toward the end of May, she said: "I'd like to go down on you. Would that be okay?"

Wow. This is something I know for certain she never did to Michael.

She started by asking me to remove my clothes and lie down on the bed. Then she held up my tie and said, "With or without? Your choice, David."

"With."

"Very well. But this time I want *you* to loosen it afterward. Do you think you can do that?"

"I'm not sure."

"If you can't, no problem. I'll take care of it. But I'd like you to try."

"I'll do my best."

"Great. As for what I'm about to do, would you rather close your eyes, or watch me?"

"Watch you."

She propped my head and shoulders on pillows. Then said, "Ready?"

I was.

She tied the knot, positioned the washcloth under the rope, then tightened it and gave me the best—well, obviously it was the best blowjob of my life, but that doesn't begin to describe what I experienced. More powerful than any drug rush you could imagine, this was a screaming high that scaled the very Olympiad of ecstasy.

I cried.

I literally cried.

And yes, she had to loosen and remove the tie from my neck or I—no doubt in my mind—would have died that day. And I was so grateful she saved me, and so sexually spent, and so emotionally dependent on her affection that I curled up in a ball beside her and cried for joy. And Nicki held me close to her body and placed little kisses on my cheek and neck, and told me how much she loved me. It honestly broke my heart when she said it was time to leave.

"This was a good day," she said.

As I got dressed and left the hotel it dawned on me that Nicki had been right all along. Her version of sex was worlds better than anything I'd experienced or seen in movies or read about in books. She was guiding me, step-by-step, into a world I never knew existed. One that had always been there, but was never appreciated. Like those contestants on *Naked and Afraid XL*, where they go to some God-awful place and try to survive for 40 days with little food and water. And when they're done they get to take a simple shower— you just know they have a deep appreciation for that shower! — and all their senses are engaged, and a common shower becomes a spiritual experience.

Nicki was a spiritual experience in her own right. Add the tie and her incremental approach to giving me more and more of herself with each visit and you've got a prescription for paradise. What I interpreted as her craziness or possible insanity during our first date, including the slap, turned out to be a poor judgment on my part. The truth is Nicki has a precise, orderly mind, and when you allow her sexuality to unfold at her pace, and accept and trust her without hesitation, the rewards are infinite. I found myself living for the Tuesday phone call, and needing Friday like a drug addict needs his next fix.

Each visit with Nicki was like a game of chess played at the highest level, where every move brought me closer to taking the Queen. And finally, after many weeks, she allowed me see her completely naked. And that's when she told me how to unlock "a person's" phone and delete "a person's" photos. She also hoped she could trust me not to copy those photos onto my own phone, and of course I promised not to, knowing full well I was going to break that promise, because honestly, how would she ever know?

As I dressed to leave she said, "Promise you won't get jealous or angry when you see the photos. Try to remember that was a different place and time, and I only did it then so this could happen now."

"I won't even look at them."

"Yes you will. But when you do, take a moment to study my facial expressions and you'll be able to tell how much I hated doing that. But what helped me get through it was knowing it would keep me in the game long enough to get you interested."

"I know how hard that was for you, and I'll take it for the compliment it is, and won't get jealous."

"Thanks, David."

Chapter 17

IT'S NOT LIKE Michael disappeared during the seven weeks Nicki and I had been hooking up. He was barely surviving, pouring himself into his work during the week, spending his weekends moping around his apartment or at our house. It was obvious he was using illicit drugs to cope with the pain of losing Nicki, and though we were growing annoyed with his inability to move forward, Alison and I gave him as much encouragement as we could.

Of course Michael made Jessie's life miserable. Every few days he'd ask about Nicki and pump her with questions about where she was or what she was doing or who she was seeing. This, because Jessie's the only family member Nicki has called since early April. But Jessie refused to tell him anything more than Nicki was fine, she had a secretarial job somewhere in Colorado, and wasn't dating anyone yet, far as she knew.

Fridays with Nicki were the best times of my life, and saying goodbye was the worst. But this particular Friday I couldn't wait to get home, knowing Michael would be there soon, knowing within hours I'd have a dozen pornographic photos of Nicki to sustain me for the six days I wasn't able to see her each week.

That evening I offered to take Michael and Alison out to dinner. While they were getting ready I sneaked into Michael's room, found his phone, and hoped he hadn't changed the security code Nicki provided.

He hadn't.

From there it was a simple matter of locating the photos and transferring them to my phone, then deleting them from his. Wham, bam, thank you, ma'am! Unlike Michael, I protected Nicki's photos with a separate security code: my date of birth.

The following Tuesday I was very proud to announce: "The photos you were worrying about have been removed forever."

She couldn't contain her happiness. "Thank you, David! This calls for a celebration. By the way, from now on I'd like us to meet at my place. But you can't tell anyone where I live, okay?"

I nodded.

"I'm renting a house in Shelbyville, so it's a bit of a drive for you."

"No problem."

"I'll want you to rent a car each week, wear a ball cap and sunglasses, and arrive as close to noon as possible. When you turn into my driveway I'll open the garage door so you can drive right in. Then I'll close the door before you get out of the car. That way no one will see you."

"I appreciate that."

"It's just a matter of protecting your privacy. This only works if it's safe for you."

Actually, it would have worked for me whether safe or not, because if Alison or Michael found out, I'd still want to see Nicki every week. If Alison wanted a divorce I'd buy a house and ask Nicki to move in with me. But yes, I *did* appreciate all the care she took to protect my marriage. As she said months earlier, she loves Alison. Yes, she's fucking Alison's husband, but she still considers her a friend.

Wait: did I just say Nicki and I were fucking?

It's true. That was the celebration Nicki was referring to on Tuesday after I told her I erased the photos.

What was it like to finally make love to Nicki? Incredible? No, better than that: it was everything I dreamed it would be. And she was totally into it: no vomiting, no anger. Like a great dancing instructor, she led. Like an eager student, I followed. She showed me what she liked and didn't like, and what worked for her; and guided me through the process with great care and affection. And after a few clumsy missteps on my part she made it clear I finally understood how to bring her the maximum pleasure possible.

But much as I enjoyed the lovemaking, nothing compared to the erotic stimulation she performed as I stood on the stool with the—are you ready for this? —hangman's noose around my neck.

Until Nicki came along, I'd never even *seen* a hangman's noose, much less held one. But she actually taught me how to *tie* one!

As she coiled the rope that first time she said, "There's a long, storied history of hanging, and a proper rope is the product of numerous considerations."

"Like what?" I asked.

"The victim's height and weight, the height of the tree branch or beam, and the intended purpose."

"Isn't the purpose to kill the victim?"

"Ultimately, yes. But do you want him to experience a humane, instant death, or do you want him to suffer the torture of the damned for several excruciating minutes? Do you want to disembowel him as a lesson to others, or humiliate him by making him shit and piss himself in front of his friends and loved ones while gasping and flopping about like a fish on a stringer?"

"It's a gruesome business," I said.

"It can be."

I resisted the urge to ask why we were tying a hangman's noose and how she knew so much about them.

"The knot is placed under the left ear," she said, "and your body weight, plus the force of the fall is usually sufficient to break the neck. The noose is designed not to jam, while being virtually impossible for the victim to loosen, even if he manages to get his hands free."

As she wrapped the coils she said, "Each coil adds friction to the knot, which makes it that much harder to loosen. Six to eight loops on a sturdy, natural rope is sufficient to kill anyone." She finished the knot, then tested it, and handed it to me.

"Impressive," I said.

When I handed it back, she untied it, then handed me the rope and said, "Your turn."

It took me several tries to win her approval, at which time she continued her lecture: "Long drops kill you instantly, breaking your neck, tearing your internal organs, causing them to leak through your lower...openings. Everyone urinates and defecates after a long drop hanging. Conversely, while the short drop also tends to cause involuntary shitting and pissing, it's more likely to occur with women and girls. In Nazi Germany the soldiers enjoyed humiliating girls by making them stand on buckets with a tight noose around their necks. When the bucket was kicked away the girls would gasp and convulse for several minutes while urinating and soiling themselves. The soldiers thought that was particularly gratifying to watch, as it discouraged others from hurling rocks or insults at them."

"That's...horrible."

"Standing on a platform with a noose around your neck is very dangerous, David. It's something you should never do with or without someone close by that you can trust to save your life if something goes wrong. Do you understand what I'm saying?"

"Yes."

"This is serious stuff. Welcome to the big time!"

She pointed to the thick wooden beam in her den and said, "My plan for today is to throw this rope over that beam and tie it off. Then you'll stand on a stool naked and I'll place this noose around your neck and tighten it. Then I'll pleasure you. When you're done, I'll do everything I can to save you. But you're twice my weight, and this is an 8-coil noose. It will be very hard to open. What I'm saying, you'd have to be an idiot to do this. But from what I've read, the payoff is other-worldly: like graduating from cocaine to heroin, but better: because the noose engages every aspect of your mind and body. It will be everything you've experienced with the slip knot, plus five times the danger. So: Are you in or out?"

"In."

She grinned. "God, I love you!"

"I love you too, Nicki. Swear to God!"

Chapter 18

AFTER THE HANGMAN'S noose, there was no going back to the slip knot or anything else we'd ever done together. From that day to this she gave me a choice between making love or being stimulated while hanged, and I always chose the noose.

I was hopelessly addicted.

Don't get me wrong: sex with Nicki was as good as sex gets. But I could get sex elsewhere, if necessary. If not Alison, perhaps one of our social friends. Or, last resort, a hooker. But where on earth would I ever find a gorgeous young woman who's willing to hang me in her home while stimulating me to orgasm, and who can be trusted to save my life?

One Friday, after several weeks of earth-shattering orgasms using variations on the noose, Nicki placed a small box on her dining room table and surprised me by saying, "Would you like to give me anal today?"

"Seriously?"

She nodded.

"I'd *love* to!"

"I figured you'd say that. And I want you to know that I love you enough to let you do it to me. Except...I think it's only fair you should have at least a small idea what I'll be experiencing. Which is why I bought this."

She opened the box and showed me a strap-on penis and said, "It took me forever to find one this small, but it's your exact size." She giggled. "I'm sorry. That didn't come out the way I meant it." She giggled again. Then said, "I'm very happy with your size, David. You're just right, as far as I'm concerned, and if you were bigger our lovemaking would be far less pleasant. What I meant to say was most people who buy these things apparently want giant ones. So anyway, I found one your size, and if you want to give me anal, it's only fair that I do it to you first. Is it worth it to you to take it in order to give it?"

I took a long time before answering yes. And when I did she wasn't overly pleased, but said, "Okay, then. I've never done this before, but I've been reading about it and the key appears to be adequate lubrication. I also recommend we focus on the method that affords the least pain for most people."

"I agree. Which method is that?"

"You bend over a table or some other object that's approximately waist-high. And the other person...well, you know."

We looked at each other a moment. Then I nodded, assumed the position, and let her lube me up. When she strapped on the penis I said, "Be gentle."

"Always, darling."

Was she? I couldn't tell. It was agony. And then it occurred to me we hadn't set ground rules regarding time. With each thrust I tried not to scream, but it dawned on me she's hammering me with a dildo, which means she's never going to "finish." After about six minutes of soul-sapping pain I said, "I don't want to break any rules."

"I appreciate that," she said, and kept thrusting. Then added, "Did you have a question?"

"Yes."

"Please ask it, then."

"How long were you intending to do this?"

"I feel it should be the same amount of time you're going to do it to me."

"How long has it been so far?"

"Twenty-eight seconds."

"*What?* That can't be right."

"I set a timer when we started. Want to see?"

"Yes. After."

"Have you had enough yet?"

While I considered her question she continued thrusting the dildo into me, harder than before, and I realized she was trying to get me to quit. That way she wouldn't have to do it as long. But since this might be my only shot, I wanted to maximize my upcoming experience with her. So I said, "Let's stop at the one-thirty mark."

"Are you sure?"

"Yes."

When it was over, she showed me the timer and said, "How bad was it?"

"Brutal. I swear, when you told me twenty-eight seconds, I thought you'd been at it more than six minutes!"

"Great," she said, with a total lack of enthusiasm. "But fair is fair, and now it's your turn."

She pulled down her pants and panties and assumed the position, but just as I was about to go for it I said, "Nicki, it was a lot more painful than I expected. I don't want to hurt you. I'm going to give you a pass."

She stood up and turned to face me. "That's not how it works, David. If you refuse to do this, it will set our relationship back. And neither of us wants that. Come here."

I moved closer, and she hugged me and said, "I think it's really sweet of you to say, but—and I'm being serious now—don't ever do that again. I wouldn't have offered myself if I wasn't 100% willing to do it. I just wanted to make it less pleasurable for you."

"What do you mean?"

"I always knew you had a fantasy about giving me anal, and you proved it today by agreeing to take it up the ass in order to do it to me. But until today I've resisted because anal intercourse is *not* a loving gesture. It might give *you* pleasure, but it can only give me pain. So I wanted you to experience the pain, even though I wasn't able to experience any pleasure, since for me it was nothing more than pushing a latex mold into you. Based on your comment, you probably won't derive the same amount of pleasure you were expecting because you've realized your fantasy was personal, selfish, and never took my feelings into consideration. Now you're aware how badly you're going to hurt me, and I think that might diminish the experience for you."

"I'm certain it will." Talk about a buzz kill!

"Good." She turned her back to me and assumed the position. "So this is for you, David. Please keep an eye on the timer. That's all I ask."

The first issue was getting hard enough to make it happen. I was so concerned about hurting her I couldn't get it up at first. But the view she presented made it impossible to remain flaccid forever, and then I had to cope with how incredibly tiny she was compared to me. And that's when I realized what she knew from the start: how terribly unfair the experience would be for her. But she braced herself and I finally worked my way in, and soldiered on. She tried as hard as she could not to make any wounded puppy sounds, and just as she predicted, the next 90 seconds weren't half as pleasurable as I originally fantasized...and yet...dare I say it? It was still awfully damn good! So good I had to remind myself to wipe the grin off my face when I finished. I'll give myself credit for not going in as deep as I could have, and for only moving enough to stay erect. But when it was over and I saw the tears streaming down her face it broke my heart, and soon I was crying, too.

"I love you," I said, but she said nothing.

I added, "You taught me something very profound today about love. It's a lesson I'll never forget."

Again she said nothing, and we got dressed in silence. Moments later I left her house shamed and filled with self-loathing.

Chapter 19

THE NEXT WEEK when she opened her door I could tell she'd
been crying.

"What's wrong?"

"You're gonna be mad at me."

I felt my shoulders sag. Shit! I knew at once she was planning to
end the relationship.

"I won't be mad, Nicki. Disappointed? Yes. Heart-broken? Almost
certainly. But not mad."

"I hope not, but I have a feeling you will be. And you're probably
gonna hate me, too."

"Don't be silly. You're my treasure, Nicki. There's nothing you
could say or do to make me hate you."

"I'm pretty sure that's not true."

I sighed. "Can we sit down and talk about it?"

"I'd like that."

Nicki's rental house was small. The kitchen, dining room and
den were all areas of the same room with no walls to separate them.
We sat on the couch, and I couldn't help but look above me to see
the beam she hanged me from as recently as two weeks ago. Now that
seemed like a distant memory.

"Tell me what's happened."

"Nothing. It's just time."

"You're ending it?"

"Yes."

"Are you sure?"

She nodded. "Yes. I'm sorry."

"Is there someone else?"

"No. It's nothing like that."

"Then...what's wrong?"

"We need to stop."

"Why?"

"It's not right."

"But that doesn't make sense. Just last week you told me how much you loved me."

"I still *do* love you, David."

I took a moment to try to work it out in my head. "You seemed fine on the phone Tuesday. You talked about taking Jessie to the concert Wednesday night, and I did what you said, I stayed away so you wouldn't see me. And I know Jess had a wonderful time."

"It's not about the concert. Jessie's great. We had the best time ever."

"Then...it's about our anal session last week."

"No. I mean...in a way, yes, but it's more than that."

"Honey, I know I hurt you last week, and I'm so sorry. I told you then that you taught me a valuable lesson about love, and it's true: you made me a better person. You'll remember I offered not to do it, but you insisted and said our relationship would suffer if we didn't. And even so, I tried as hard as I could not to hurt you."

"I know. You were wonderful. You've been wonderful the whole time. But we need to stop."

"Why?"

She sighed. "I feel compelled to mention you're breaking the rule about walking away when one of us says it's over."

"All due respect, I don't give a flying shit about the rules right now, Nicki. I love you, and I'm fighting to save us."

"Let's not end things on a sour note, David. We've had a great run. I think you'll admit it's been a lot of fun."

"No doubt. But—"

"And surely you knew it couldn't last forever."

Suddenly it became clear to me: this is what Nicki *does*! It's what she did to Michael over and over. She breaks up, takes some time alone, then comes back. Sure, she explained that away by saying she kept going back to Michael to be with me, but what if it's more than that? What if she just gets overwhelmed by relationships after a few months and needs a break?

She says, "Did you really think this was going to last forever?"

"I *hoped* it would. And I still believe we can get it back."

"We *could*, but you won't want to."

"Of *course* I want to! I'm not the one trying to end things. I love you, Nicki! You understand that, don't you?"

"You say that now, but things change. Except for my love for you. That will never change." She sighed. "I'm gonna miss our time together, David. Not so much the sex part, but all the attention and love you gave me. That's something I'll never forget as long as I live."

I took a deep breath. "Something obviously happened to change your mind. The only thing I can point to is the anal situation. I know you hated that, and when I left last week I felt just awful. Every day I wanted to call and talk to you about it, but I didn't want to break your rules. Then Tuesday finally came and I asked you several times if you were okay, and you said yes."

"I already knew on Tuesday we were gonna end things today. But I wanted to do it in person, and didn't want it to affect being with Jess on Wednesday."

"Maybe you just need some space. How about we take a two-week break and see how you feel then?"

"David, look at me. It's not about *me* needing a break. I'm doing this for *you*. You're the one who's going to want to stop seeing me."

"That makes no sense. I've never given you *any* indication I want to end things, and I certainly don't want to do it *now*. I've *lived* for these Fridays, Nicki. You've changed my whole outlook on life."

"It's been really good for me, too, but—"

"I've done everything you asked. I was patient with you, loving, and kind. I adore you, Nicki. And you keep saying you love me, too."

"I do. I'll always love you."

"Then...what gives? Why break us up? I know you keep saying it's time, but why *now*? Why not next week or next year?"

"I finally have everything I need."

"What does that even *mean*?"

"Our anal experience was the last piece of the puzzle."

"What puzzle?"

"Maybe this will help me explain." She picked up her remote control, aimed it at her giant screen TV, pressed a button, and a video started playing.

It took a brief moment for my brain to fully comprehend what was taking place on the TV screen: Nicki was pegging me in the ass. I watched in stunned silence as the scene played out, and then I watched me doing the same thing to her.

She turned off the video and said, "I've been filming all our sessions with multiple cameras, and they're all are quite compelling. But this one goes above and beyond, don't you agree?"

"Don't I...*what*? What's this all about? I...have no idea what's going on. You've been so careful every step of the way. So protective of me. Why the fuck would you—"

"There's a financial component to what we've been doing."

"You...need *money?* Jesus, Nicki, all you had to do was *ask!* Whatever you want or need, just say the word and it's yours."

"Thank you David. That's very sweet of you. How does two million dollars sound?"

Chapter 20

"*EXCUSE* ME?"

"It's a small number," she said.

"You're...*blackmailing* me?"

"Don't be silly. I'm simply giving you a chance to do the right thing."

"You've been leading me on all this time so you could shake me down for two million *dollars*? What're you planning to do, show this video to Alison if I don't pay up?"

"We said we wouldn't mention her name again. Or Michael's."

"Fuck your stupid, fucking rules! You've been setting me up all this time? Ever since you started dating Michael?"

"I *said* you'd be mad, but you said you wouldn't."

"Are you for *real*? Hell yes I'm fucking mad. Wouldn't *you* be?"

"I don't know. It hasn't happened to me yet. If it does, I'll let you know."

"I assume you're filming all this. Are you purposely trying to piss me off, hoping I'll hit you or something? Wait: if you *are* filming this you're providing video evidence of blackmail."

"I'm not filming this part."

"So if I decide to beat the shit out of you there's no way you could prove it."

"That's right. But when I recover the price will double."

"What if you *never* recover? What then?"

"You'll go to prison for murder. I've had a whole week to make copies and put them in safe places. Not just here, but in my safety deposit box. Plus, I have a friend who's holding one in case something happens to me. I only showed you a small clip, but the video's two hours long. Call me pessimistic, but I think it's gonna make you look bad."

"I don't have two million dollars in liquid assets."

"That's okay. I'm not in a rush. But the sooner you pay me the less it's gonna hurt."

"Why's that?"

"If you don't pay up in seven days I'm going back to Michael. I'll be part of the family again, and they're gonna wonder why you're acting so weird around me."

"You'd do that to my *son*? *Use* him like that?"

"Michael loves to be used. As I said before, I only went back to him to get to you."

"And *this* is what you meant?"

"Partly. But I've always loved you, David. That's not gonna change."

"You're insane!"

She sighed. "See? This is why I said earlier you'd want to stop seeing me."

I gave her a look. "I'm trying to understand. Are you saying you'd continue seeing me if that's what I want?"

"Yes."

"But I'd have to pay you two million dollars for the privilege."

"That's correct."

"Would you expect more money down the line?"

"No. I think two million's fair."

"Oh, you *do*, do you?"

"Yes. I'm not greedy."

"Would it come with a guarantee?"

"What do you mean?"

"For two million dollars I'd like a long-term relationship."

"I think we've gotten off track. What I'm saying is you're gonna pay me two million dollars whether we see each other or not. But if you still want to see me after that, I'm willing to try, because I love you. But if we're being practical, it only seems likely you're gonna come out of this experience with bitter feelings."

"Ya think?"

"Yes. And if you change our relationship or change the way you treat me I'll probably want to end things."

"If I pay you two million in cash, you're willing to keep fucking me. Is that what you're saying?"

"No. Because I would never put it that crudely. But I would continue our sessions as if nothing had changed."

"Right. And again, just to be clear, if I don't come up with the money in seven days you're going back to Michael?"

"Yes."

"And you're going to use him."

"That's correct."

"You're not a very nice person."

"Don't be mean."

"Really? Don't be *mean*? Let me tell you how this is going down, Nicki: I'm not paying you shit. If you show your tapes to my wife, or anyone else, I'll have you arrested for blackmail."

"I'm pretty sure that can't happen unless you record me threatening you and demanding money. Otherwise it'll look like we've been having an affair all these months and you broke up with

179

me and I was so hurt I decided to punish you by showing Alison what you did."

"I'm not going to pay you."

"I think you will."

"In case you haven't noticed, my marriage isn't all rose petals. I expect we'll divorce when Jessie goes to college in two years anyway. But if it means saving two million dollars, I'm willing to break the news to Alison today."

"I see."

I smiled. "Face it, Nicki: you swung for the fences, but took your eyes off the ball. Extortion's not for amateurs. You're in over your head. I should be furious with you, but I'm willing to consider this an aberration in an otherwise excellent partnership. I'm willing to put this behind us and continue seeing you, on two conditions. Want to hear them?"

"Yes."

"You'll have to give me all copies of the tapes you made, and you're going to have to agree to some changes."

"Like what?"

"Like from now on I'll make the rules."

"Such as?"

"You're going to see me at least twice a week. You're also going to take my calls whenever I choose to make them, and you're going to keep me informed as to where you are and what you're doing every day. You'll not be allowed to see other people, and you'll tell me your plans for us in advance, and I'll tell you if those plans are acceptable."

"And in return?" she said.

"In return I'll pay you...twenty-five hundred dollars a month. How does that sound?"

"Light."

I laughed. "I'm willing to entertain a counter offer."

"I appreciate that."

"Very well, Nicki. What do *you* think is fair?"

"Two million dollars. And if you want to keep seeing me it will have to be on the same terms as the day we began the affair."

I shook my head. "Have you been listening to me at *all*?"

"Yes. And I don't appreciate the tone, *or* the content."

"I've made you a fair offer. And I agreed to increase it. Within reason, of course."

"You made me a *whore's* offer, and a cheap one at that. You're willing to throw away everything we built because of a measly two million *dollars*?"

"Are you listening to yourself?"

"You're trying to turn our relationship into something you could get from a hooker!"

"Not true: a hooker wouldn't try to blackmail me."

She said, "Until now our relationship has been based on love and respect. You said I taught you a valuable lesson about love."

"Yes, and now you've taught me a valuable lesson about blackmail."

"The lesson's not over, David."

"What do you mean?"

"I didn't want to get into this if I didn't have to, but...there's more to this than you think."

"Like what?"

"I have a backup plan."

She stood, walked to the bathroom, came back holding some cotton swabs and three plastic zip lock bags. Then she took one of the cotton swabs and rubbed it against the inside of her cheek, and placed it carefully in the zip lock bag and handed it to me. The label on the bag said *Nicki*.

"What's that for?"

She handed me a couple of swabs and the other plastic bags, one of which was labeled David. Then she said, "Nicki Hill's my pretend name. My real name's Katie Walker."

"So?"

"Think about it."

"Why? Is that name supposed to mean someth—"

My stomach lurched. I jumped to my feet, then vomited.

"*Jesus*, David!"

I puked again. I couldn't help it. When I finally had the strength to speak I said, "This isn't funny. How do you know about that?"

"Because I'm Katie."

"That's impossible. Total bullshit!"

"Sorry to break it to you David. I know you haven't heard that name in 23 years, but it's the name you gave the hospital so no one could trace me back to you and Mom. I'm your daughter. Your first born. And that swab contains enough DNA to prove it."

Chapter 21

"YOU CAN'T POSSIBLY be...I mean...This can't be true."

"I understand it's hard news to hear, but you'll come to accept it over time."

"What the fuck is *wrong* with you?"

"Nothing. I mean, you didn't have any problems with me before today."

"You've...you *fucked* me? Your own *father*? And fucked your *brother*?"

"You know I did, so there's no need to be so dramatic about it. To you it's a big thing. You know why?"

"Yes. But clearly *you* don't. Jesus *Christ!*"

"Don't act so superior. Let's not forget how much you loved the sex. You certainly loved it more than *I* did."

I shook my head. Nothing made sense.

She went to the kitchen, got a large plastic garbage bag and a roll of paper towels and brought them back to the den. She got down on her hands and knees and started cleaning my mess off the hardwood floor. I tore a few paper towels off the roll, took them to the kitchen, ran some water on them and brought them to the den, got on my knees and began washing the areas she'd cleaned. As we worked, she said, "You got Alison pregnant and gave me away."

"We were *children!* We weren't even married!"

"Oh, please. You got married a few months after I was born. You could have gotten me any time you wanted, but instead you and Mom decided to start a new life without me. I was shuffled from one foster home to the next, and each was worse than the one before, because the older I got the more things they could do to me."

She inspected the floor carefully, then stood and got a mop and some disinfectant from her laundry closet, and finished cleaning the floor while I took the garbage bag to the garage and placed it in her trash can. I came back to the den as she finished up, then waited while she put the mop and disinfectant back in the closet.

When she reentered the room she said, "They usually placed me in a home where the foster parents had one or two kids, and sometimes other foster kids. And you know what the men always told me the day I moved in? They said, 'I'm going to be like the father you never had, so don't call me Rick. Don't call me Frank. Don't call me Jim. Don't call me Bennett.' They all said, 'Call me Dad.' And they introduced me to their sons and daughters and the other foster kids and said I should think of them as my real brothers and sisters. But you know what happened? The fathers and sons usually found a way to get me alone. While you and Alison were creating your perfect little family I was getting serial raped by grown men."

"I—look. I know it was hard on you. But that doesn't justify tricking Michael and me into having sex. It's unnatural. It's...*perverted.*"

"Are you kidding me David? I've been fucked by so many fathers and brothers in my life you and Michael are just one more set. The only difference is I genuinely care about you."

"You're sick."

"If I am it's your fault."

"Your mom and I were young. We couldn't take proper care of you."

"You can tell yourself that all you want, but it's not true. You had Michael, your little prince, less than two years after abandoning me. And you kept him. Fine. I could've accepted that. I mean, I certainly wouldn't have wanted you to give up your own son. But let's fast-forward six years: by then your business had taken off and you were making money hand over fist, and you looked around your perfect little kingdom and decided something was missing. What could it be? What could make your world even better? And then it hit you: a little girl! But Alison didn't want to go through another pregnancy, so after spending a lot of time and money you adopted Jessie.

"*Adopted* her!"

I sighed. "This sort of talk isn't productive."

"I was still out there, David, only eight years old, worrying all day what might happen to me after the last lights were turned off. Your perfect little family required a cute little girl? Well guess what, *Dad?* I was a cute little girl! I mean, I only have a couple of photos to prove it, but if you saw them I don't think you'd accuse me of being a *beast.*"

For the first time she looked like she might cry as she said, "You guys wanted a sweet little girl, you could have adopted *me.*"

Chapter 22

"I GET THAT, Nicki. But you're right: we *didn't* adopt you. And now you're punishing me for it."

"Like I said, I'm giving you the chance to make it right. Two million dollars won't bring back my innocence. It won't give me the childhood I never had. It won't allow me to have children of my own someday...but it could help me have a future."

I let her vent some more before saying, "I'll make you a deal: if the DNA results prove conclusively that you're Katie, I'll pay the two million. But you'll have to agree to move away and never contact our family members again."

She shook her head. "Why am I not surprised to hear that your solution to 'what should we do with Katie?' is to banish me from your family again, while not bothering to consider I *am* your family?"

My turn to vent: "You want to know why? I'll *tell* you: it's because you didn't knock on our door eighteen months ago and say, 'Hi Dad, I'm Katie, your long lost daughter.' Instead, you seduced your biological brother and used him to get closer to me. Then you seduced *me*, your own *father*, and got me to participate in the most disgusting sexual acts imaginable. I don't even think there's a *word* for what you've done. It's the most degenerate thing I've ever heard of! The highest possible degree of perversion."

She looked at me as though seeing me through different eyes. Then, very calmly said, "You're a hypocrite, David. And by the way, there *is* a word for what I've done, and it's a common one. It's called incest. And here's something interesting: I don't recall *ever* hearing you define our relationship as perverted until today. Thirty minutes ago you couldn't get enough of me. For the better part of a year you wanted to be *inside* me. And when I finally let you, you felt like you'd died and gone to heaven. Well maybe you hate to admit your own daughter gave you the best sex of your life, but it doesn't change the fact I'm the exact same person I was thirty minutes ago when you offered to do anything to keep our sexual relationship alive."

"You find that strange? That I could enjoy having sex with a woman right up to the moment I found out she was my *daughter*? And she knew it all along?"

"Yes. I *do* find that strange. Because in our case, daughter is just a title. It means nothing. You're 42, I'm 23. We never saw each other till last year. You fell in love with me. And whether you want to acknowledge it or not I'm still the woman you wanted to have sex with as recently as noon today. You were willing to leave Mom for me!"

I stared at her in disbelief. Then lowered my voice and said, "You knew what you were doing. You knew I'd be repulsed to hear the news. You counted on it. It's the reason you taped us having sex. It's the reason you knew I'd pay you the money. So don't bullshit me about how being my daughter is only a title. You've heard my terms. Take it or leave it."

"I'll take it. But you might want to climb off that big white horse, because ten minutes ago you offered to pay me twenty-five hundred a month to keep the relationship going. The same relationship you now claim was perverted. But over the years, as your net worth kept rising, five million, ten million, twenty million, fifty million, and counting... you never once picked up the phone to try to find me. You'll pay twenty-five hundred to fuck a pretty 23-year-old every Friday but you won't pay ten cents to help your own daughter get some clothes, food, or medical treatment after getting an abortion from her rapist. I waited my whole life for you to find me. But you never even tried. You think I'm perverted? Think about this, David: in my whole life the only way I was able to get your love and affection was to let you fuck me."

She took a deep breath. "You've got seven days to pay up, or I'm going back to Michael. And when he brings me to visit the family, you're going to be the same David you've always been as far as Alison and Jessie are concerned."

"And if I can't do that?"

"I'm afraid I'm going to insist that you do."

"Help me understand why it's so important for me to pretend I want you in my house, knowing you're just waiting to be paid."

"Because despite what you think about me, all I ever wanted was to have a real family. Remember last Christmas?"

"What about it?"

"That's the only time I've ever experienced being with a real family at Christmas. And everyone liked me and wanted me there because I was Nicki, not Katie, and I was so happy, and I remember thinking I can't keep living with Michael because we're not compatible, but if you had told me then that all I had to do to be a part of your family was to fuck you every Friday, I wouldn't have waited. I would have done it right under the Christmas tree, and once a day thereafter. Because that's all I ever wanted. But fucking you didn't make me part of the family, it pushed me further away. Yes, I got to be with you, and two days ago I got to spend time with Jessie at the concert, but I knew my time with Michael and Alison was done. So yes

I'm going back to Michael, and I'm gonna try as hard as I can to get him to bring me to see you, because whatever time I get to be with you guys is the only time I'll ever have with you for the rest of my life."

"That's quite poignant, but let's not forget you're willing to take two million to stop being around us."

"Yes. But not being around you was your idea, not mine. And I accepted your terms because—once again—you don't want me anywhere near your family. And the two million you keep whining about is a drop in the bucket for you, so please don't insult me by acting like it's a hardship."

"I'd prefer you don't come to the house. I'm not sure I can be convincing."

"I'm afraid you don't get to make that decision. It's my last chance to spend time with my family, so if I can talk Michael into bringing me, you'll be civil or I'll tell your precious family who I really am. And I'll make sure they get copies of the video, so they can see all the degenerate, perverted things you did to your own daughter. And by the way, those are your words, not mine, because I'm not ashamed of anything I've done with you, because love is love. And just so you know, I would have done a lot more."

I decided not to tell her she's mentally disturbed. It wouldn't make a difference. Mentally disturbed people don't know they're disturbed.

She looked at me and said, "I'm sorry it has to be this way."

"Me too."

She put her hand on my shoulder. "Do you need a moment?"

I nodded, placed the plastic bags in my pocket, took a seat on the couch, covered my face with my hands and reviewed everything she said about how Alison and I let her slip from our lives and never bothered to find out what happened to her. And you know what? Everything she said about us was true. I think what happened, we felt so guilty bringing her into the world and giving her away that we convinced ourselves it was for the best, and that she was happy somewhere with a nice family, and it wouldn't be fair to take her away from that life.

But as Nicki would say, that's a copout. Because Alison and I never had a single conversation about Katie in all these years. We simply put her out of our minds. She was part of the system, and we had our own lives to lead.

I finally said, "If we'd known what you were going through all those years, we would have done something."

"I believe you. But you still should have checked."

I couldn't argue the point. We weren't wrong to let her go, but we were monsters for ceasing to care.

Nicki agreed to keep her throwaway phone and I agreed never to text her. I told her I'd call to let her know the DNA results and coordinate the payment, if it came to that. Then I said something that surprised both of us and revealed how selfish and insensitive I truly am: "If the tests come back negative," I said, "can we resume the affair? I'm willing to double my offer."

She said, "You are one sick puppy, David. And by the way, I saw you grinning on the tape while you were giving me anal."

We said our goodbyes and I started to leave, then said, "I'd feel better if you gave me a second swab."

She showed me a sad smile and said, "That's why I gave you the extra bags: I knew you wouldn't trust me. Would you like to do it?"

"If you don't mind."

"Go ahead. It only works if you're convinced the process is fair and accurate."

She opened her perfect mouth and I swabbed her inner cheek and placed it in one of the extra plastic bags. Then I took them home, made some calls and found a lab that does DNA testing. Unfortunately, they told me it could take two months to get the results. Nevertheless, I swabbed myself, placed it in the bag labeled David, and took all three bags to the lab.

Eight weeks later the results were in, and as Maury Povich would say, "David, when it comes to 23-year-old Nicki Hill, you *are* the father!"

Chapter 23

WELL OF COURSE I had to pay Nicki the money. It's one thing to tell
Alison I had an affair with our son's ex-girlfriend, but quite another
to say "The tapes you're about to see will show me butt-fucking our
birth daughter!" Nor would I want her to learn *Michael* had carnal
knowledge of his actual sister, and nor would I want Michael to know.
Or Jessie. Or any of my friends and business associates.

Nicki was right: I *did* want to stop seeing her. What's really
fucked up is before I threw my fit, she would have been willing to
keep seeing *me*! This young lady might be beautiful, but she's as
mentally deranged and sexually damaged as a person can be. I believe
she latched on to me and Michael for no other reason than because
we were the family she never had. I'd bet money she would have been
willing to have sex with Alison and even Jessie, had the opportunity
presented itself.

While I waited for the DNA results, Nicki made good on her
promise to go back to Michael, and I was dismayed to hear him
say they were talking about getting married. Her willingness to use
him knew no bounds. Yes, I could have stopped it by paying her the
money immediately, but how stupid would I feel if she wound up

clipping me for two million dollars and all I had to show for it was three cotton swabs?

The one thing I'm thankful for is she hasn't talked him into bringing her home for a visit yet. That said, they're planning to come next weekend, but she'll be long gone by then, since I'm wiring the balance of her money tomorrow.

I miss the affair.

Don't get me wrong, I'm glad it's over. It's just that I miss the "being in love" part. All those months with Nicki gave my life purpose. Something new and exciting to look forward to every single week. Now that she's gone, I'd be bored to death if not for the other thing she gave me:

An addiction to erotic asphyxiation.

Of course, it's different doing everything without a partner. First, it's more dangerous: am I going to get caught? Am I going to lose consciousness and strangle myself? It's scary, but as Nicki used to say, that's a big part of the allure.

Second, I had to find a different stimulus. While porn can never match a live sexual partner, it's an acceptable substitute for those willing to elevate the risk factor. In that regard I learned that by adapting Nicki's slip knot I could create a method that would allow me to save my own life after orgasm: by holding the knot in my teeth, I can actually loosen it at the moment I'm getting off. And it works every time. Sadly, when something works every time it ceases to be dangerous. And even though my orgasms are intense, they're nothing compared to what I experience when I'm convinced my life is truly in danger.

And so I've started taking more chances, just to—you know—make it more interesting. I stopped holding the knot in my teeth, which means after achieving orgasm I now have to turn my head and grab for it, and if I miss, I'm that much closer to death. Believe me, this is far harder than it sounds, since I'm gasping like crazy, trying to breathe, while trying to turn my head in order to grab a moving lifeline with my *teeth* that I can't even see!

But as dangerous as *that* was, after a few tries I became proficient at it, and so I had to come up with a way to step up my game. I decided to *purposely* miss the lifeline on the first try.

And that nearly did me in.

But it was so exhilarating I continued to do it that way for weeks. Now, once again, I've mastered the move, and so the danger has minimized. So today I'm going to purposely miss the lifeline *twice*.

Can you just imagine?

Two weeks ago I cashed in a mutual fund and wired $1.2 million to Nicki's account. Since then I liquidated a couple of stock positions, but the bank made me wait ten days before wiring the money from my account to hers. So tomorrow I'll wire her the remaining $800,000 and she'll break up with Michael, move away, and she'll become part of my past, and Alison and Michael will never know what happened. Meanwhile, she's leading Michael on, pretending their relationship is better than ever.

So here we are: it's a cold November Wednesday, and Alison and Jessie have left for the afternoon. I've tossed the rope over the beam in my den, tied it off to a sturdy doorknob, turned on my porn, tied the slip knot, placed the rope around my neck, positioned a towel under the rope just like Nicki taught me, so I won't show any burn marks.

Now I tighten the slip knot as far as I dare, and focus on the porn while standing on the stool and stroking myself, and...

Part Four:

Nicki Hill

Chapter 1

Present Time

SO HERE I am in Alison's hotel room, experiencing the very definition of irony: I'm getting a severe tongue-lashing by Alison while sitting on the same bed where I tongue-fucked her underage daughter fourteen hours ago.

Aside from that, her lecture's pretty similar to the one David gave me two months ago, except that instead of paying me two million to walk away from Michael, Alison's gonna pay me five million to walk away from Jessie.

As I watch her rattle on and on about what a horrid child I've been I find myself wondering what she'll do after getting her share of the inheritance. Will she sell the house and move away to make it harder for Jessie and I to hook up? Will she dump David's insurance agent or marry him? And how will she react if she catches Jessie and me seeing each other? Because there's no way in hell I'm going to give Jessie up if she wants to keep seeing me after I tell her I'm Michael's sister.

Call me optimistic, but I don't think it's gonna matter to Jessie. After all, she and I are completely unrelated. Yes, I fucked my biological brother. But when I explain I only did that so I could eventually be with *her*, I think she'll be moved, just as David was. And why shouldn't she be? It's true. And if Alison had the hots for me instead of the others, I would have stayed with Michael just to be with *her*. My point is, I love them all except—not so much Michael—and if sex is their preferred currency, it's easy enough for me to give. That's because I don't look at it the same way most people do. To me it's like anything else you'd do to make your loved ones happy. I don't enjoy sex, but I'm willing to do it to be with the person or people I love. It's like getting a job to support the family. You might hate the job, but you'll show up every day for eight hours and do the best job you can because you love your family.

So why did I have to go after David? Why couldn't I just stay with Michael and give him the sex he wanted?

That would have solved all my problems. I could have spent a lifetime of weekends and holidays with the Thornes if Michael had been a different person. But sadly, he bears an uncanny resemblance to the foster father that treated me with excessive cruelty and killed my best friend. Much as I love the Thornes, I couldn't get past the trauma of letting Michael touch me.

So my current plan is to tell Jessie immediately, and if she no longer wants to be with me, I'll contest David's will and force the family to pay me my rightful share of the inheritance.

And I'll take my chances that number will be north of five million.

Hold up: Alison just agreed to pay the full five million!

In return, I'll have to move away, stop seeing Jessie, and never contact the family again.

Obviously, the payment to me is contingent on her getting the full accidental death benefit. This, because they'll need a ton of money to pay inheritance taxes and attorney's fees.

So I'll stay cool till I get the money. I'll tell Jess we have to stay apart for a couple months, she'll ask why, and I'll tell her the whole story. Except for the part about how I seduced her dad. If she ever found out about *that*, I'd lose her in a heartbeat. Lucky for me I was extremely careful throughout the affair. The only one on earth who has any evidence linking me to David sexually is me.

Will Jessie wait for me? I sure hope so. She isn't family, but she's the closest thing I've got.

Chapter 2

Three Weeks Later

MY PHONE RINGS.

"Nicki? It's Alison. We've hit a wall."

"What do you mean?"

"According to Mr. Blass, the insurance company's going to deny the accidental death benefit. If they do, he thinks David's other policies will follow suit. Accordingly, I can't pay you the full amount."

"What are you talking about?"

"Our agreement."

"Which agreement is that?"

She pauses. "I offered you five million dollars to walk away, and you agreed."

"Actually, I agreed to accept your offer of five million dollars in lieu of contesting the will."

"Well, however you want to phrase it, if the insurance won't pay, I can only give you half."

"That seems a bit light."

"Two-point-five's a lot of money. And you already received one-point-two from David."

"Why won't they pay the accidental death benefit?"

"I don't know. It's a lot of gibberish, far as I'm concerned. But Mr. Blass is here. If you want, I'll put him on speaker."

"Thanks. I *would* like to talk to him."

"Nicki? Hi. Arthur Blass. I've been working the insurance claim for Mrs. Thorne."

"I know," I say, thinking that's not the only thing he's been working.

"The insurance company's taking the position that Mr. Thorne's death wasn't an accident because a reasonable person would understand that putting a noose around his neck for the purposes of sexual gratification could result in his death."

"It wasn't a noose. It was a slip knot. And a reasonable person would also understand that crossing a city street could result in his death."

"Yes, but the company feels a reasonable person would understand the risk difference between hanging himself and crossing a city street."

"Is the company claiming this was a suicide? Because that would go against the coroner's report, from what I've heard. Not to mention the police report."

"No. They're saying it doesn't qualify as a payable claim based on the policy provisions."

"Can I ask you a question?"

"Shoot!"

"If I tried to run across a busy highway to save my dog and got hit by a car and killed, would the company pay the accidental death rider?"

"Yes."

"And I assume that's because I didn't intend to get struck by a car?"

"That's correct."

"So is the company's saying David *intended* to strangle himself?"

"Yes. Not to death, but partially, enough to cut off his air. That's the whole point of autoerotic asphyxiation."

"Did you hear yourself just now? You said it was David's intention to partially cut off his air. Not to strangle himself to death. Therefore, his death had to be an accident."

He's quiet a moment. "You make a good case. Perhaps you should hire an attorney to present that argument."

"Why would *I* hire an attorney?"

"Sorry. I meant Mrs. Thorne."

"This is pretty clear cut, Arthur: the fact that David's death occurred because of his sexual preferences or gross negligence doesn't prevent his death from being an accident. David didn't want to kill himself, he wanted to experience an intense orgasm. If he wanted to kill himself he wouldn't have placed a cloth under the rope, wouldn't have gotten naked, wouldn't have watched babysitter porn. Yes, he knew it was a risky activity, but so is driving a car on New Year's Eve. And yet reasonable people do it every year."

"Your point's not lost on me, Miss Hill. I happen to agree with you. But as for your automobile example, the safest drivers have the fewest accidents. And David wasn't practicing safe sex when he died."

"The safest drivers get struck by unsafe drivers every day. Reasonable people know this, but it's a risk they're willing to accept. And I'm sure David understood the risks of his sexual activity."

"Well, there you have it: you've just identified the problem we're facing: according to the insurance company, there's no evidence David ever attempted this type of activity before. If he *had*, and had *survived*, they might be forced to reconsider."

"Why's that?"

"If David had survived the activity in the past he'd have every reasonable expectation to survive it the day he died."

"Didn't Alison tell you she caught him doing it?"

"Yes, but she's not prepared to take a polygraph."

"They can't *make* her."

"No, but if a wife actually saw her husband performing autoerotic asphyxiation, why would she refuse to take a polygraph about it?"

"Doesn't matter. The company's not gonna pay just because she passes a polygraph."

"No, but it might help them believe her story."

"What about *me?*" I ask. "I saw David with a noose around his neck."

"No offense, but Alison doubts that story. And anyway, sitting on the closet floor with a noose around your neck isn't the same as hanging yourself for sexual gratification."

"From what I understand there was no evidence David's death was probable, expected, or a natural result of his activity. He did it for the sole purpose of getting off, and had every expectation he'd come out of the experience alive, without injury, as he had many times before."

"Well, as I said, if there was a shred of credible evidence David had done this at least once before, we could probably get the company to reconsider."

I think about my two-hour video, and how I recorded all of David's erotic asphyxiation episodes including the one where he did every part of it himself, from tying the knot to saving himself after the fact. That's the only one that would count, but Blass said one was enough.

I ask, "If someone could prove David had done it before, how much would his family stand to benefit?"

"If all David's policies paid the accident benefit, it would add more than seven million dollars to his estate, tax free."

"Wow. Too bad there's no credible evidence."

Alison joins the conversation: "Are you sure about that?"

"What are you suggesting?"

"I think you know a helluva lot more than you're saying. I've known David all my life. There's no way he came up with this hanging thing all by himself, and there's no way he gave you all that money hoping to have an affair with you."

"We've had this discussion before, Mom, and my answer's not gonna change."

"Are you willing to accept two-point-five million to walk away? You'd also have to agree to stop seeing Jessie."

"I have no idea what you're talking about with regard to Jessie. I haven't seen her since the funeral. But since you've lowered your offer to two-point-five, I'm going to respectfully decline. I'll contest David's will and sue his estate for the portion that's rightfully mine."

"I see. And does that mean you're going to keep seeing Jessie?"

"Again, I have no idea what you mean."

"You had sex with my daughter!" she yells. She starts yelling something else, but I can't hear her over the loud banging on my front door.

Now a man's voice shouts, "Nicki Hill? Shelbyville Police Department. We have a warrant to search the premises. Would you mind opening the door?"

I open the door to see Detectives Broadus and Rudd, and four policemen. Broadus hands me a piece of paper and says, "Miss Hill, this is an official search warrant issued by Derrick Compton, Magistrate, District 1, Shelbyville, Kentucky. Please stand aside and allow the officers to do their job. We'll try our best to make this as quick and painless as possible, but we expect your full cooperation." To the officers he says, "Be sure to confiscate her computer and any electronic devices." Then he asks for my phone. Before turning it over I hear Alison shout: "Rot in hell you fucking bitch!"

Chapter 3

I WASN'T STARTLED by the police.

Moments earlier, while talking to Mr. Blass, I heard a slight beep and walked to my bedroom and lifted a single wooden slat a quarter inch so I could peer out my window undetected. The reason I knew someone was in my driveway is because I'm in the same house in Shelbyville that I rented last April, before David and I began our affair. Back then I installed a driveway alert so I'd know when he pulled into my driveway each Friday. That way I'd be able to open the garage door for him.

When I looked out the window moments ago I saw two sedans in my driveway and one on the street in front of my house. All three appeared to be standard police issue, but the one on the street looked exactly like the one I saw three weeks ago at the Thorne estate: the one that belonged to Detective Broadus.

There was no need to panic then or now.

I've been expecting them for weeks.

Broadus says, "Would you consider answering some questions? It would save us having to take you down to the station."

I laugh. "Which station is that? The one in Lexington?"

Detective Rudd smiles.

Broadus says, "Are you going to talk or not?"

"Let's sit at the kitchen table."

The three of us sit down and I say, "Go ahead and ask your questions, and I'll consider answering them."

"Very well. You understand we're just doing our job."

"Of course. What would you like to know?"

He presses a button on his phone and says, "Do I have your permission to record this?"

"Yes."

He tells the recorder the date and time, who we are, why they're here and gets me to give him permission. Then says, "How many times has David Thorne been inside your house?"

"This house?"

He nods.

"To the best of my knowledge, he's never been in this house."

"Either he has or he hasn't. Which is it?"

"As far as I know he had no clue where I lived. Neither did any of the Thornes."

"Then your answer is?

"I don't know."

"Why's that?"

"As I told you three weeks ago, David was determined to have an affair with me, but I turned him down because—as I'm sure you know—I'm his biological daughter. But David didn't know that, and so he pursued me. As you also know, David was quite wealthy, and it's possible he hired a private detective to locate me. If so, he may have been stalking me without my knowledge. If so, he may have broken into my house when I wasn't here."

"Have you reported any break ins to the local police?"

"No."

"So can I assume we're not going to find any of David's clothing, toothbrush, or personal effects today?"

"I wouldn't assume anything. Maybe the men searching my home will plant something. Maybe David planted something after breaking in."

"Why would David break into your home and leave evidence?"

"I have no idea. But this is the same guy who broke into Michael's phone and stole my photos."

"Have you seen any of Mr. Thorne's personal items in your house?"

"No. And by the way, I'd be shocked if you found a single skin cell or hair follicle that belongs to David."

"Why's that?"

"Because he's never been in this house, as far as I know."

"We think he has, and I'll tell you why: For six straight Fridays David drove to Frankfort and rented a car and drove precisely 45.8 miles before returning it."

"*Precisely* 45.8 miles? Every single time?"

"Close enough."

"How close, exactly?"

"Within a range of two miles over six different Fridays. So you know what we did last week?"

"You drove from Frankfort to my house and back and logged precisely 45.8 miles?"

"Bingo. How do you explain that?"

"I'd call it a mild coincidence."

"Mild?"

"If you start by assuming he went to the same place every Friday there might be a hundred possible destinations that total 45.8 miles' roundtrip, including virtually every house in this neighborhood. Since my house is one of them, I'd call that a mild coincidence."

"And if we find some of his personal items or DNA today?"

"That could only happen if David or the officers planted it."

Detective Rudd says, "I can't help but notice you've got three sturdy beams in your den."

"Maybe you should check them for rope fibers."

"Good idea. Too bad it's not on our search warrant."

Broadus glares at him.

I say, "You have my permission to search the beams for rope fibers."

"We do?"

"Certainly. You *do* understand this isn't my house, right? And that I'm just renting it? I have no idea if the owner or any of the other tenants ever hanged themselves on those beams, but that would be *another* coincidence, don't you think?"

Broadus says, "Three weeks ago you said you put a million dollars into a mutual fund in Michael Thorne's name."

"That's correct."

"Can you provide us with that information?"

"It's in my purse. Want me to get it?"

They look surprised. Rudd says, "Please."

I locate the piece of paper that contains the fund's name, Michael's account number, and all the prompts and passwords.

Broadus looks at it and frowns, then hands it to Rudd.

"Mind if we call them?"

"Suit yourselves."

Rudd takes out his phone, punches in the numbers, and after a few minutes of dealing with the automated phone prompts he gets a human on the phone who verifies the account, the balance, and the sole owner: Michael Thorne.

"When did you open this account?" Broadus asks.

"The day after David wired me the money."

He tells Rudd to hand him the phone. Rudd does, and Broadus asks the rep for the date the account was set up and the amount of the initial deposit. Then he hangs up.

"Satisfied?" I say.

"No."

"Why not?"

"You told Alison Thorne you lied to me about setting up this account."

"Did I?"

"According to Mrs. Thorne, you told her you kept the money for yourself. You said if you had put it into Michael's name you would have had to pay the gift taxes and wouldn't have had the money to do that."

I shake my head. "I love Alison, but I think between David's death and finding out that I'm the daughter she gave away at birth, she's been through a lot. I think it's taken quite a toll on her."

"So you're saying you never told her that?"

"That's what I'm saying. But even more to the point, why would I tell her I kept the money for myself when clearly I had given it to Michael weeks earlier?"

"Good question, and here's another: why haven't you told Michael?"

"I did. In fact, you were right there in the hotel lobby when I told him."

"But you haven't told him since then. According to Michael, you've never identified the account."

"Well surely he admitted the $200,000 was in the joint checking account."

"He did. But why haven't you given him the mutual fund information?"

"We haven't actually been speaking. But when we do, I'll be glad to tell him, or *you* can, if you like. Meanwhile, the money's sitting there, building up value for him. And if he hasn't received the first monthly statement by now I'm sure he'll get it soon, since I put his address on the account."

"With Michael out of the picture, how do you intend to pay the gift tax on the initial wire transfer?"

"I was hoping to inherit money from my father's estate."

"My understanding is, you made a five-million-dollar deal with Mrs. Thorne."

"That's correct. She offered me five million not to contest the will or sue the estate. But a few minutes ago she rescinded that offer, so I guess I'll have to sue."

"Why did you give Michael the money?"

"I trusted him. At the time, I thought we were going to get married."

"According to Mrs. Thorne, you had sex with her underage daughter."

"I know."

"Excuse me?"

"She told me the same thing on the phone just now!"

"What's your response to that accusation?"

"It's the first I've heard of it. Like I said, I think the strain of David's death has gotten to her. First she claimed I lied to you and kept the money for myself. Well, you just cleared that up, didn't you? Then she claimed I had sex with her daughter. Surely you asked Jessie if that's true."

They say nothing, which tells me what I already knew: there's no way in hell Jessie would rat me out. When I told her I was Michael's sister she didn't bat an eye. She's tough as nails. And, she's in love.

I laugh.

"What part of this strikes you as funny?" Broadus says.

"Think about it: I've been accused by Alison of having sex with everyone in her family except her."

"You knowingly had sex with your biological brother."

"I wouldn't call it having sex, and I doubt he would, either."

"You certainly lived together as a romantic couple. Why?"

"Michael and I were like roommates. If you ask, he'll tell you we were never officially engaged. That's just a story I agreed to let him tell people so they'd stop bothering him about it. But I couldn't be engaged to him or have sex with him. Like I said, I'm his *sister*. I never told him that, but I wanted to. I just never found the words."

"That's a load of bullshit."

"Well, of course there's more to it. I never had a family of my own, so I gravitated to Michael and accepted his affection...to a point. But I was going through a lot of personal stuff, and—you know the expression 'any port in a storm?' —That's what Michael represented to me."

"Mrs. Thorne says you used him to..." He stops in mid-sentence and shakes his head. "Oh, never mind. She destroyed her credibility with the mutual fund thing."

"I'll admit I stayed with Michael longer than I should have, but I did it so I could be around my real family."

"Why didn't you just tell them who you were?"

"Can you imagine how awkward that would have been? They didn't want me, Detective. If they had, they would have located me and invited me into their lives. But they didn't, so I had to force the situation. I wanted them to meet me as a stranger, with no preconceived notions. I knew they hated all of Michael's former girlfriends, so this was my chance to see if they would like *me*. And they did. They loved me."

Rudd says, "We never stopped working the blackmail angle. But since you gave the money to Michael before we began the investigation, it's going to be hard to get any traction." He looked at Broadus. "Can we turn off the recorder?"

He does, and Rudd says, "You know what I think? I think David had the hots for you and when you broke up with Michael he saw an opportunity, made his move and you told him you couldn't have an affair with him because he was your father. And I think he felt bad about leaving you all those years ago, and wanted you to have something, so he sent you the cash."

Broadus says, "Wrong and wrong. Because if that was the truth, she wouldn't have had to transfer the money to Michael. But she *had* to."

"How do you know?"

"Because no one's going to give up $1.2 million if they don't have to."

Rudd says, "It's going to be hard to prove it."

"Not if we find evidence linking her to sexual activity with her father."

"You won't," I say.

"Because you clean up well?"

"Because there isn't any."

Chapter 4

THE OFFICERS REMAINED in my house nearly four hours, and never found any evidence of David.

Like Detective Broadus said, I clean up well.

From the minute he and Rudd claimed they were terminating the investigation I knew they were lying and hoped to lull me into a false sense of security. So that very day, after getting my stuff from Michael's apartment, I washed all my clothes, threw away my bed spread, sheets, pillow cases, all the items inside my refrigerator and closets, and scrubbed every surface in my house. I washed all the silverware and every dish and glass and all the pots and pans I own. I even got a ladder and wiped off all traces of rope fibers from the beams. I cut both ropes we used into one-foot pieces, and dumped them in gas station trash cans and dumpsters all over Louisville. I bought a new laptop, threw away the old one (after removing the hard drive and drilling holes in it with an industrial strength drill Michael had in his utility room). I also destroyed and threw away the video recorders and the pieces of both copies of the videos I made that chronicled my sexual activities with David.

After talking to Alison in the hotel that day I told Jessie who I was, and said the only reason I'd remained with Michael was so I could get closer to her. I said I intended for us to be together, though it couldn't be right away. She said she'd wait for me till her eighteenth birthday if she had to, but no longer. I told her it might very well be that long, but said I'd be in contact as soon as I was convinced the police had concluded their investigation.

Then, even though I was convinced all traces of David were removed, I hired a cleaning crew to clean the house from top to bottom, including all surfaces, light switches, wall plugs, light bulbs, appliances, and I supervised their efforts. Two days later, I hired another cleaning crew to do the same.

As it turned out, Alison and Arthur Blass were lying about the insurance company denying the accidental death claim. Their call was a sting operation. She had called Detective Broadus to report I was her biological daughter and told him I'd been having sex with Jessie. Then they put their heads together and came up with the idea of trying to get me to come forth with evidence that David had performed his autoerotic activities previously. This, because Broadus was still convinced I had seduced David and blackmailed him into sending me the money. The plan was for Alison to call me on the phone even while the police were ready to surprise me with a search warrant. No doubt Alison was hoping to get two things from the phone call: a confession about being with Jessie, and evidence of David's sexual activity that I could only provide if I had, in fact, been sleeping with him. Alison hoped I'd be put in prison, and she'd be able to keep Jessie from my clutches and the family could move on with their lives.

But I managed to stay several steps ahead of them. The very day Alison and I had our talk in her hotel room I set her up by claiming I kept the $1.2 million for myself. I knew if she planned to shaft me, she'd use that to get Detective Broadus's attention. And I also knew it would hurt her credibility once I proved I never kept the money.

Why didn't I keep it?

Too risky. It might have been construed as blackmail. Before David killed himself my plan was to live with Michael and never tell him about the $1.2 million, much less the other $800,000 David still owed me. I was going to withdraw the gains on that mutual fund over time, along with some of the principal. With any luck, Michael would live his entire life without knowing about the money, because I controlled it. After all, I had the password and account number, not him.

But when David died, all my plans went up in smoke. And when Jessie revealed her intentions I discovered I really cared for her. And by the way, she stands to inherit a fortune of her own, so that opens the door to lots of possibilities.

As for Alison's sting, and the police raid, I saw it coming a mile away. I've never trusted the police. Not only that, but Jess told me her mom confronted *her* about us. So we devised this plan: Jess told her if I really did say those things I must have been fantasizing it. She then offered to prove she was still a virgin. Alison said, "I'm happy to hear that. But it doesn't prove you weren't molested." To hedge her bet, she forbade Jessie to ever see me or speak my name again. Then last week, one of my neighbors informed me that a police detective asked him if he'd ever seen me with a man that matched David's description, or if he'd ever seen the various rental cars David had driven to my house those weeks.

My neighbor told them nothing. He hates the cops more than I do.

So anyway, Alison tried to set me up. And you can say anything you want about me, but she's the real villain in all of this. She's the one who gave me up at birth. What sort of mother doesn't want her own child? She's also the one who treated David with indifference. After giving her the most amazing life a woman could ever hope to have, she treated him like shit and had a long-term affair with his married insurance agent. She also cussed me out in the hotel and said she'd seen enough of me for a lifetime. Then she tried to slap me. Then she forbade Jess and me to see each other...and finally, she tried to set me up with the cops.

Everything Alison has was given to her by my father, and now she stands to inherit the bulk of his estate, even though she's been cheating on him all this time. This bitch never worked a day in her life, never earned any portion of what she now has, or what she stands to inherit. Most importantly, she hasn't had to suffer a day in her life!

Because of that, and because of how she tried to fuck me over, I'm gonna have to punish her. I won't do it immediately, but rest assured Alison Thorne is gonna have to deal with me some day, after everyone's forgotten about these events.

Chapter 5

Two Years Later

ALISON PULLS INTO her driveway shortly after ten p.m., having enjoyed a night out with friends. She parks her car in the garage, enters her house carrying a wedge of birthday cake, and sets the alarm. She places the cake in the refrigerator, then walks to her bedroom, thinking she's alone in her giant house.

But she's not.

As she enters her closet to change into her pajamas, a large man comes up behind her and puts his hand over her mouth and drags her back into the bedroom. He throws her to the floor, pins her down, puts a knife to her throat and tells her to shut the fuck up.

It's not hard to find men such as these. Times are tough for many, and evil people are a dime a dozen if you know where to look.

As he proceeds to brutally rape her she hears a light tapping at her bedroom door, and a woman's voice says, "Happy birthday. I love you."

She knows the voice is mine, and that her nightmare is just beginning.

THE END...But Please Keep Reading!

Author's Note:

AS I MENTIONED earlier, I met a woman who claimed to be the real-life Nicki.

I've been asked but won't reveal if I paid her for telling me her version of the story, and here's why: if I *didn't* pay her you'd question why she was willing to tell me so much; and if I *did* pay her, you'd question her veracity. So let's just say she was very forth-coming for reasons of her own. She's the one who told me the rumor about Alison being sexually assaulted for nearly six hours on the night of her 40th birthday, and I took the considerable liberty of adding the "artistic touch" that the perpetrator was hired by Nicki herself, which I'm sure will piss her off if she ever reads this account. Likewise, the tapping at the door was my creation, and if it didn't happen that way, I feel as though it should have.

Those of you familiar with the true story will certainly question my stating as fact that Nicki Hill had a full-blown affair with her biological father. That was widely believed, but never proven, though Nicki herself claimed it happened, and took full credit for introducing David to the world of erotic and autoerotic asphyxiation.

Another note about my "artistic" ending: although I believe 90% of Nicki's comments, she's not the most reliable source I could hope for, and I have to confess that Alison never reported the six-hour ordeal she allegedly suffered at the hands of Nicki's hired goon. For this reason, it's possible the prolonged assault may not have actually occurred. However, her children and closest friends are convinced *something* of consequence happened that night, as she refused to be seen by anyone—including her housekeeper—for three-and-a-half days. Nor would she accept phone calls. And while she never spoke of any sort of incident, her daughter Jessie says her mom was never the same after that night.

While I've done extensive research on the real-life characters who populate this story, there's a limit to what I can reveal without compromising their privacy. But I *will* tell you this much:

Detectives Broadus (retired) and Rudd (active):

I have no updates to share with you on these guys because, quite frankly, I didn't want them to catch wind that I've been poking around in their old case. Broadus was a bulldog investigator, and I'd just as soon not have to explain how much I know or how I obtained the information (He's recently retired and has too much time on his hands!) I do know he and Rudd never found any physical evidence that David Thorne had ever been present in Nicki's rental home, and therefore the 45.8-mile rental car mileage discovery (which I considered brilliant) was not something they could positively link to her. That said, I'm sure if you asked Detective Broadus he'd say he's convinced to this day that Nicki had an affair with her biological father and attempted to blackmail him as a result.

Arthur Blass:

I seriously wanted to refer to Mr. Blass as Mr. Balls and had to fight the urge to do so. This, because in real life the man's unfortunate name is closely linked to male genitalia, and that's all I'll say about that! I know for a fact that Alison relied heavily on Mr. Blass to help her get the insurance company to reverse their initial in-house denial of the accidental death portion of the claim. From what I gather he convinced them that between Alison's considerable wealth and highly-connected political friends, the company would almost certainly get "home-towned" if they found themselves in court trying to justify their refusal to pay the claim. After making several unsuccessful attempts to settle for a lesser amount, the insurance company finally held its nose and wrote the check.

Arthur Blass didn't fare nearly as well. Hopelessly in love with Alison, he asked his wife of eight years for a divorce, and she fought him tooth and nail and wound up with a large chunk of his net worth, including their house. As he removed his tools and other personal effects from the garage cabinets, he overlooked a quarter that had fallen to the floor (I originally wrote "shiny" quarter, but I have no proof of its condition). But what makes the quarter important is Mr. Blass had previously installed an expensive coating to the surface of his garage floor that made it easy to clean, but quite slippery when any object such as a dog bone, ink pen, or piece of pocket change gets caught under a person's shoe. Blass slipped on the quarter, hit the back of his head full force, suffered a stroke, and died either two or three days later, depending on whether you believe the coroner's report (two days), the obituary (three days), or the family's recollection (three days). I don't have a clue why there's a discrepancy about the man's date of death, and to be honest, I don't care enough about it to pursue it further.

Alison Thorne:

Apart from what may or may not have happened to her the night of her 40th birthday, Alison's life is still pretty cozy. She obviously never married Arthur Blass, because even in Kentucky it's considered poor form to marry a dead guy (though it's not without precedent). She inherited an undisclosed sum that's rumored to be in excess of $60 million, and occupies a portion of her weekly hours by serving on charity committees.

I know you want more details, but she's pretty high profile, and I don't need the legal hassles. But I will say this: if you were to ask me if in real life Alison is a well-known breeder of horses (not personally, but through her affiliation with a well-known horse farm) I won't dispute it.

As I revealed earlier, when I attempted to contact Alison, her attorneys threatened me with a lawsuit. I pretended to be intimidated, to keep them from filing a cease-and-desist. After giving her kids the impression I hadn't started writing this story and was, in fact, backing away from the project...everything quieted down. I put out the word I was working on my next Western to throw them off the scent. And now—if you're reading these words—you'll know I was able to publish this book before they thought to get an injunction to prevent it.

Alison, if somehow this book makes its way into your hands and you tell your socialite friends it's unflattering and one-sided, well... you had your chance to go on the record, and didn't. I certainly would have given you the opportunity to tell your side of the story, but no, you decided to unleash your attorney hounds on me. That said, I think we both know the account I've written in these pages is awfully close to the truth. As for the alleged birthday assault, I would have treated you fairly: you could have simply denied it or refused to comment, and I would have printed whatever you chose to say.

Michael Thorne:

Michael helped Nicki's reputation by downplaying their previous public displays of affection and denying any sexual activity occurred between them. Like Nicki, he claimed they were basically roommates, and though they occasionally "kidded around" in public and had seen each other in various states of undress in his apartment, they slept in separate bedrooms and never engaged in any form of sexual activity. For purposes of this story, I stuck with Nicki's account, since to me it passes the smell test (and makes for a better story!) All jokes aside, the detectives were so convinced Nicki and Michael engaged in sexual activity they stated it as a fact in their final report.

Michael claims he was never head-over-heels in love with Nicki, and disputes her assertion that he pressured her to marry him. He was extremely pissed at me for reporting her claim that he raped her the night of his father's death. He called me an "asshole," a "filthy piece of shit," and refused to write a blurb for my book cover. But he did verify my educated guess he inherited approximately $10 million from his father's estate.

Despite his harsh feelings for me, I found Michael to be well-adjusted, and more intelligent than Nicki made him seem. I was pleased to learn that shortly after their final breakup, he met a nice southern debutante from a legacy family, married her, and continues to live in the same city I described as Lexington, Kentucky. As I write these words, they're expecting their first child, a daughter, whose imminent arrival should precede the publishing of this book (I decided not to ask if they planned to keep her!)

Jessie (Jess) Thorne:

Alison was right about Jessie and Nicki's relationship. Despite her promises to the contrary, Jessie's feelings for Nicki crashed and burned long before her 17th birthday. I'd tell you Nicki's version as to why that happened, but it's pretty far-fetched and self-serving compared to Jessie's. Then again, if you know anything about Nicki, her calling card is that nothing that ever happens to her is her fault.

Although Jessie refused to discuss her personal relationship with Nicki, according to one of her close friends (who wishes to remain anonymous), Jessie was never in love with Nicki, but developed a crush on her during a time in her adolescence when she was confused about her sexuality. According to the friend, Jessie and Nicki's sexual play never progressed beyond a PG rating (again, I sided with Nicki's version because it makes sense Jessie would downplay her sexual involvement to her friends. That said, I *do* believe the part about the crush versus Nicki's insistence that Jessie loved her deeply. I think Nicki was probably projecting).

About six months after her father's death, Jessie met a guy and fell in love and they dated throughout her senior year of high school. After graduating they attended different colleges and are no longer seeing each other. Jessie says her inheritance matches Michael's, however, she disputes that the sum was "approximately ten million." She claims it was "closer to eight", though she concedes Michael might be including the $1.2 million Nicki transferred to his account.

My discussions with Jessie were phone-only, but based on her numerous Facebook photos I can verify her looks are every bit as striking as Nicki portrayed them in our meeting. She, too, seems well-adjusted, and her future appears secure.

Nicki Hill:

Despite all that happened, I can't help but come away with warm feelings for Nicki. The worst abuses she claimed to suffer in foster care apparently did occur (though I couldn't find any evidence to support her claim that one of her foster fathers murdered anyone, much less another foster child. Nicki attributes this to a police cover up, but that's simply not true. When I asked her to tell me the girl's name she claimed she couldn't remember. And yet it was supposed to be her "best friend" at the time. So I know for a fact that part of the story was embellished. Nevertheless, I took the time to investigate it, and I did find that one of her foster fathers sexually assaulted and severely beat one of the girls in his care, and she spent two days in a hospital. Though her injuries were listed as "severe" they weren't at any time down-graded to "life-threatening." Still, I'm sure it had a traumatic effect on Nicki, who was living in the house at the time).

Two of Nicki's foster fathers were arrested. One served (and is currently serving) time for crimes against children (he's the one who beat the young lady in question) and the other is a registered sex offender. Although she may have embellished a few details, Nicki's stories are generally true, and horrific, and anyone who can move forward from that sort of abuse is okay in my "book." I obviously don't condone everything (or hardly anything) she did, but in my heart I believe she got a raw deal from her shitty parents, David and Alison, and I can understand why she felt betrayed. I also understand *why* she did what she did, after gaining an understanding of how she interprets sexuality as currency, and how she seems able to mentally divorce herself from societal conventions.

Nicki refused to say how she learned so much about erotic asphyxiation, and when I try to picture how she gained that knowledge my mind goes to a dark place. She asked if I ever tried it and I jokingly said "No, but you sure make it sound like a good time!" That's when she told me something interesting that happened the first time she used the hangman's noose on David (I didn't put it in the main story because I thought it would be more interesting if I revealed it here, after the fact).

She said at one point David's knees buckled on the platform and his body sagged and he started choking to death and "it was as if he had no bones in his legs!" She said, "I couldn't get his legs to hold his body up!" In a panic, she got her shoulder under his thighs and tried to lift him, but when she did, the noose "wouldn't open the slightest bit." Unable to get his legs working, she made the decision to let go of him, at which point "David was literally hanging to death!"

According to Nicki, she grabbed a bar stool from the kitchen and positioned it behind David's body so that the seat was about a foot higher than his butt. She worked her shoulder under his legs again and managed to get him on the barstool, which gave her about a foot of slack in the rope to work with. When she finally got the rope off his neck he told her he never lost consciousness and was completely aware of everything that happened during the ordeal, though at the time he was unable to speak or move his arms or legs. As Nicki apologized profusely, she claims David said it was the most exciting moment of his entire life and asked if they could do it again right then and there. Nicki refused, but said they did repeat the procedure a couple of times during future visits, but only after making sure the bar stool was always within arm's length.

After a long, bitter legal battle to claim what she considered to be her fair portion of her father's estate, Nicki once again came out on the short end of the stick. After legal fees she said she wound up with less than a million dollars. Both Michael and Jessie dispute that claim, saying she got closer to two million before attorney fees and the gift taxes the IRS forced her to pay. After all expenses, they believe she netted about...get ready for it...*one-point-two million dollars!*

—And that's the truth!

Thanks for reading my book!

John Locke

7/13/16

Personal Message from John Locke:

I love writing books, but what I love even more is hearing from readers. If you enjoyed this or any of my other books it would mean the world to me if you'd click the link below so you can be on my notification list. That way you can receive updates, contests, prizes, and savings of up to 67% on eBooks immediately after publication!

Just access this link: http://www.DonovanCreed.com and I'll personally thank you for trying my books.

Also, if you get a chance, I hope you'll check out my friend Dani Ripper's website:

http://www.DaniRipper.wordpress.com

John Locke

New York Times Best Selling Author

Guinness World Record Holder for eBook Sales!

8th Member of the Kindle Million Sales Club!

(Members include James Patterson, George R.R. Martin, and Lee Child)

John Locke had 4 of the top 10 eBooks on Amazon/Kindle at the same time, including #1 and #2!

...Had 6 of the top 20 books at the same time!

...Had 8 books in the top 43 at the same time!

...Has written 30 books in five years in six separate genres, All best-sellers!

...Has been published throughout the world in numerous languages by the world's most prestigious publishing houses!

...Winner, Second Act Magazine's Story of the Year!

...Named by Time Magazine as one of the "Stars of the DIY-Publishing Era"

Wall Street Journal: "John Locke (is) transforming the 'book' business"

John Locke

New York Times Best Selling Author
#1 Best Selling Author on Amazon Kindle

Donovan Creed Series:

Lethal People
Lethal Experiment
Saving Rachel
Now & Then
Wish List
A Girl Like You
Vegas Moon
The Love You Crave
Maybe
Callie's Last Dance
Because We Can!
This Means War!

Emmett Love Series:

Follow the Stone
Don't Poke the Bear
Emmett & Gentry
Goodbye, Enorma
Rag Soup
Spider Rain

Dani Ripper Series:

Call Me!
Promise You Won't Tell?
Teacher, Teacher
Don't Tell Presley!
Abbey Rayne

Dr. Gideon Box Series:

Bad Doctor
Box
Outside the Box
Boxed In!

Other:

Kill Jill
Casting Call
When David Died

Kindle Worlds:

A Kiss for Luck (Kindle Only)

Non-Fiction:

How I sold 1 Million eBooks in 5 Months!

Made in the USA
Middletown, DE
03 March 2017